The Journey is My Home

Also by Lavinia Byrne

The Daily Service Prayer Book
The Life and Wisdom of Augustine of Hippo
The Life and Wisdom of Benedict
The Life and Wisdom of Catherine of Siena
The Life and Wisdom of Francis of Assisi
The Life and Wisdom of Francis of Xavier
The Life and Wisdom of Margaret of Scotland
The Life and Wisdom of Teresa of Avila
A Time to Receive

The Journey is My Home

LAVINIA BYRNE

Hodder & Stoughton

LONDON SYDNEY AUCKLAND

British Library Cataloguing in Publication Data
A record for this book is available from the British Library

ISBN 0 340 75692 6

Typeset by Avon Dataset Ltd, Bidford-on-Avon, Warks

Printed and bound in Great Britain by
Clays Ltd, St Ives plc

Hodder & Stoughton
A Division of Hodder Headline Ltd
338 Euston Road
London NW1 3BH

Contents

Introduction

This is a story about a journey. I write it warmly, thanking God who makes journeys possible. I have no desire to be adversarial, to condemn named individuals. In one sense I write as a bystander to my own journey. Bits of it I chose to make; others were chosen for me, sometimes against my own volition. When you write a book you start remembering things. In this act of remembering, of sorting out the fragments of my life and trying to reassemble them, I offer as candid a picture of this journey as I can. After all, the storyline is simple: I entered a religious community in 1964 and left it in the year 2000; I wrote a book about the ordination of women as priests in the Roman Catholic Church in 1993 and it was destroyed on the orders of the Vatican in 1997; I began writing and broadcasting in the late 1980s and continue to do both.

Obviously my own account of these events is partial. All autobiography is. There are real people whose story is tangled up with mine and whose reputation and integrity I seek to protect. The arms of the Vatican's Congregation for the Doctrine of the Faith –

the former Holy Inquisition – have a long reach and I would not like to see anyone else suffer from their grasp.

All story-telling is selective and mine no more than most. If that sounds overly defensive, there is a very good reason for it. For this is a story about a journey which I undertook in faith and freedom as a child and which has led me into conflict with the Catholic Church.

I am and remain a loyal Catholic. I am no longer a member of the Institute of the Blessed Virgin Mary, the container which held my Catholic experience for me. For the Church, through the action of the Congregation for the Doctrine of the Faith, has destroyed my vocation to that particular calling. Those are hard words to write; it has been a hard experience to live through.

What follows is an account of what happened. My account, and mine only. I thank all the people who have helped me write this book, either by encouraging me as I was writing or by reading it in manuscript form.

The title is supplied by a letter which one of St Ignatius of Loyola's first followers wrote. His name was Jerome Nadal and he was trying to say something about his commitment to the will of God to others among Ignatius's companions who were looking for permanence and stability. The Ignatian way of life could not guarantee these for them, nor for his present-day followers either, as I have myself discovered. The reality of this particular way of life – a life that is all about seeking God's will – is far more exciting than that.

1

A Garden Enclosed

'A nun is like a garden enclosed.' I heard an elderly and prestigious Jesuit priest say those words during his speech at Prize-Giving at the convent school where I was teaching in the early 1970s. It was a golden day, with bright sunlight streaming through the back windows of the rather dingy, cramped concert hall where we were gathered. The parents sat in proud and serried ranks, the dark suits of the fathers setting off the pretty frocks of their wives to perfection. In the nicest possible way their daughters oozed success. We were all on parade and knew it. I can remember the smell and the sound of the occasion: fresh soap, expensive scent, traces of cigar smoke, the gentle knocking sound of gold on gold as the women eased the bracelets on their wrists or the chokers on their necks. The priest in question was wearing a black suit and white dog collar. He stood out in the crowd and mirrored back to the nuns, also wearing black and white, everything the Church was saying to us about our status; what we could be and what we could not be.

He was a stocky man and his hands described the

image of the garden he was talking about. A garden enclosed, four-square, secure, safe. I was in my mid twenties, demurely habited, one of the smiling faces at the back of the hall, delighted that my A-level pupils had done so well. The habit was deeply flattering because it managed to make all those who wore it appear slim. White cuffs and a sharply-cut, white starched collar set off the black to perfection. We were an elite and looked the part.

Yet I listened to this man with a mixture of longing and revulsion. After all, I was a young nun and it was my life he was talking about. Was I a garden enclosed? Was I to live at one remove from reality? For I was sure that that was what he meant. Even now I can recall the feelings that went with listening to his words because this was a seminal moment, one of those snapshots you are given when you look both backwards and forwards with a strange degree of clarity. You take stock of your past and future, of your hopes and fears, and you are given a grid or frame of reference to assess them by.

I can explain both the longing and the revulsion. I can even claim to do so with some of the insight I received as the sun streamed in through those high mock-Gothic windows. But of course I know that I am projecting – as we all do – adding some insights which only came later and with age, subtracting memories I would rather forget. The past is a vast and lonely place and sometimes we wander around it ill at ease, lacking landmarks, so we concoct these to suit ourselves. We reconfigure, conflating experiences at whim, reformatting the bits which no longer fit, only allowing certain memories and consigning the rest to some mysterious recycling bin in the sky. That afternoon was a landmark moment though, and I want to try to be faithful to it, because by recalling it I can gain detachment, which is a virtue I value.

For the priest's words reminded me powerfully of my own longings. They helped me to look backwards, to consider my own aspirations when I joined the community. On one level these are easy to describe. The feelings I had had when I first began to consider a religious vocation came flooding back to me. I had a rush of idealism that recalled the generosity and simplicity which inspires any young woman as she offers herself for service in the Church through the religious life. I was transported back in time and saw myself standing on the terrace at Coxley in Somerset where I was brought up. My first true home. I know what I looked like that day as I have a 'real-time' photograph of myself taken on 8 November 1964, just before I entered the convent. Again it is a snapshot, offering a judgment, an opinion of that moment. I stand in my riding boots, jeans, cotton shirt and a woollen jumper, curly hair pushed back off my very young-looking face, determined, ready, wanting to be off. The walled garden at Coxley where I lived, with its plum trees, asparagus bed, herb garden, French-style flower and vegetable patches, is behind me, out of sight. So too is the water butt where an adder lurked which came out in the summer to sun itself on the stone path. I would torture it by spilling cold rainwater out of the butt onto its back and run off laughing to gorge myself on Victoria plums and greengages.

I knew all about walled gardens: places of enchantment and places of peril. To me they represented deep
privilege as well as withdrawal. My parents had bought
Coxley House in 1953 and I had lived a sheltered and
protected life there. I still visit the present owners and
hear again the sound of the wind in the copper-beech
tree on the drive and the click of the metal catch on
the gate. I remember that the garden at Coxley
represented summer and the lazy sound of lawn
mowers; ripe tomatoes clustering on their stems in the
little greenhouse, while hard little green grapes failed
to ripen in the big one and my pony's manure withered
at their feet. There are other memories too: these were
of garden parties where boys from Downside, my
brothers' school, lounged about in pinstriped trousers
and black jackets looking hugely desirable. They are
about loneliness, a little girl lying on the ground
reading, devouring book upon book and rolling over
to fall asleep in the hot sun.

But there was peril too. It came in different forms
when nature took its revenge and spoilt the idyll: when
the fox visited and my hens were killed, their bloodstained feathers scattered with vicious abandonment;
or summers when my asters failed to flower; scary
moments when the taunted adder threatened me with
its forked tongue. I now realise that it is hardly
surprising that the story of the fall in the Bible is set in
a garden. The early authors of Genesis knew that the
encounter with good and evil is more acutely experienced there than anywhere else. A garden looks like
paradise but it is always more than that.

So an enclosed garden was a place of chance, a

representation of a fallen world as well as a comforting one. In my imagination it will always have a double identity, Eden and the fall; God's paradise and our fool's world spar with each other to offer seclusion, retreat and, as I saw it that summer afternoon in 1975, a lie. You cannot escape human nature; you cannot run away from the human project, which is about growth, greed, diversity, desire, humanity, hellishness, love, lust and a host of other feelings. On one level I had run away from a garden enclosed when I joined the community in 1964. I had left the security of a middle-class home and family expectations about settling down and living happily ever after. I had taken the risk of grappling with good and evil, with religion, with the nature of the human self and our relationship with God. Was I now discovering in that Prize-Giving speech that I had unwittingly run towards one as well? Because of course I know – I knew – all about the desire to live safely. Yet the journey is our home. Only by travelling on do we become who we are.

I wonder now what that priest meant when he said, 'A nun is like a garden enclosed.' What was he promising to the parents that summer afternoon as their daughters walked up to receive their prizes? I felt that he was being sentimental. I felt that he was promising the parents a future which no one could deliver; that an unending stream of nicely brought up nuns would go on teaching their children and their grandchildren for ever; that the values and the Church they were to embrace were those of an enclosed world, never mind an enclosed garden. I was uncertain about my own commitment to be part of it. He wanted to take the sting out of the idea of a garden, to present it as a neat and tidy place where nothing could go wrong. He forgot that a garden is about growth and that that inevitably means change.

I was fourteen when I had first experienced God's call. It did not come suddenly; it grew slowly. I knew with absolute certainty that I wanted to be a nun. I was entranced by poetry at the time and found that Gerard Manley Hopkins captured my experiences in his poem, 'A nun takes the veil'.

> I have desired to go
> Where springs not fail,
> To fields where flies no sharp or sided hail
> And a few lilies blow.

He wrote of the 'havens dumb' which are 'out of the swing of the sea'. Not quite the same image as a 'garden enclosed' but one that is even more powerful, for it is all about enchantment with none of the exposure to peril. So its effect is the same. For what is promised in Hopkins' poem is a place of immense security, far away from the pressures which bear upon us in any form of modern living; a place where nothing hard will come, and certainly no storms; yet, I would now claim, a place of denial and subjugation of all that makes us truly human – our passions and desires, our hopes and fears, the sheer bloody-mindedness of being made in God's image and likeness, yet deeply flawed by original sin. Aged fourteen, who could not crave such an innocent and uncomplicated life? A life of

8

flight and dedication where God would be at the centre of all one's thoughts and actions, and everything else would be constellated around that central commitment. Above all, a haven, a safe place.

Hopkins was a Jesuit. In the event he learnt – as I would have to – that the religious life is not a life of withdrawal and seclusion; it could not afford him any kind of comfortable refuge from his gifts or his vision, his pathology or his sheer cussedness. When I first read his poem I found it profoundly moving and inspiring. It made me want to be a nun more than ever. At seventeen I followed my desire and joined the Institute of the Blessed Virgin Mary. My dreams came true. Now, at fifty-three, having left the order, I am as suspicious of the poem as I was when I first heard that other Jesuit priest say to the serried ranks of parents at Prize-Giving that 'a nun is like a garden enclosed'. Yet I am more tolerant both of Hopkins when he wrote it and of myself when I first heard it. I am even rethinking the man who told me that nuns were gardens – and walled at that.

Let me explain. Nowadays if you go into any decent children's bookshop, you find a section called something like 'hormonal upheaval'. Now Hopkins and I had no such aids to teenage – or young adult – living. In my own case, hormonal upheaval or teenage years were contained in an incredibly kind and charitable environment. It was also a deeply pious one. At St Mary's Convent, Shaftesbury, where I went to school in 1958, I first met the sisters of the community which I was to join. They were young, intelligent, kind, interesting women who were huge fun to be with. The building itself was spectacular. In her book, *The Best Kind of Girl*, Gillian Avery examines the girls' schools which emerged over the late nineteenth and twentieth century: St Paul's, Rodean and Cheltenham Ladies College, the North London Collegiate and other schools which continue to adorn the league tables. These were schools which took the educational project of girls' education really seriously. My headmistress was a product of one of the cluster in the Girls Public Day Schools Trust. She was a convert to Catholicism and brought with her a genuine commitment to girls' education. She spoke to us often of the duties which accompanied the advantages we enjoyed. Responsibility would come with education. It was not a private gift for an individual to enjoy; rather it was a gift to enhance the life of people around us. The messages about service which I was hearing from the Church were reinforced by those I heard at our school assemblies.

There are convent schools too in Gillian Avery's book and of mine she wrote something astonishing. She claimed that it had the most beautiful views of any school in England. I am convinced that this is true: at St Mary's, Shaftesbury, the Wiltshire Downs roll continuously before your eyes, ever-changing under fresh floods of light from the wind-blown skies. They alter in shape; they alter in scale. The promise is about growth and change, about variety and about security. From the safe home of the school terrace, you can contemplate unfathomable journeys – to the farthest fringes of the known world and to the furthest recesses of your soul.

When my parents took me for an interview to St Mary's in 1958, I sat on the window seat in the front parlour, as it was called, half attentive to the discussion which my mother and father were conducting with the Reverend Mother – about subjects and fees and whether or not I could bring my pony – but mostly attentive to the view outside the window. That Reverend Mother has since told me that the image was unforgettable: the little girl with the cloud of curly hair who was half in and half outside the room, kicking her heels on the paintwork in order to twist round and gaze at the view.

This is a landscape that says that it is all right to change and to dream and to have visions and to aspire to great things. It is a landscape which is totally unenclosed, its only boundaries being the Downs and the sky. In the event, when I arrived at school, I did so as a strange little cripple. For starters I was late. Term began in early September 1958. I rolled up a month later with a funny, shrunken white leg, newly released from a six-week stay in plaster. Sunbeam, my pony, had fallen on me heavily during Pony Club Test D up at Horrington above Wells in Somerset. I had been taken down to the local cottage hospital and told not to cry though I was moaning with pain. I only burst out sobbing when my jodhpurs were unstitched the length of the seam inside my right leg, so as to release the broken tibia, and I thought they would be ruined. How could I explain that to my mother?

The next part of the journey proved a bit of a laugh, for I was taken in an ambulance to the local mental hospital, known as 'The Mendip', and swung through its gates in style. The X-ray machine at the cottage hospital was broken, so I was momentarily the youngest insane patient in Somerset, by proxy as it were. I knew the Mendip well, as my best friend's father was a psychiatrist there. I looked through the grey frosted panes of the ambulance windows as I went past their home, trying not to feel frightened. I had played endlessly at their house in the hospital grounds as well as on the tennis courts. I had no fear of the patients and found it touching when a man who had hired deck chairs on the beach at Weston-super-Mare asked my brother to go over there and tell his wife that he still loved her.

Now the Mendip Hospital really was a garden enclosed: a magnificent nineteenth-century edifice with a Gilbert Scott chapel and tree-lined grounds. For all the world it was like an Oxford or Cambridge college with high-ceilinged rooms, views over towards Glastonbury Tor and the Somerset levels, a farm and grounds to kill for. Is it surprising that in January 2000 when I went back to Somerset having left the IBVM community, I went straight to an estate agent who was offering property up at South Horrington, or St Thomas's Village as the hospital is now called, and looked at the possibility of getting hold of a flat there? Journeys have unexpected homecomings yet this would be a comforting one for me. Madness, and my own particular madness in leaving the security of the community, seeks some kind of containment. More than that, because I actually feel quite sane, I seek healing and I know that I could find it there.

St Mary's Convent, Shaftesbury, my school, was a

strange kind of mirror image to the Mendip. The hospital was purpose-built whereas the school had been a private house – brewers' baronial in style. I was hugely happy at school and loved the way in which the chapel was accessible to me. At home, namely Coxley, two miles outside of Wells in Somerset, I had had to get up early and cycle in to Mass. My pocket money went on ice cream (three homemade cones for sixpence) and toy soldiers from Woolworths. At school I could spend my pocket money on CTS (Catholic Truth Society) pamphlets. These explained the faith to me. I also had to go to Mass and Benediction twice a week, and to the rosary, spiritual reading, night prayers, and prayers at morning assembly. All in all a lot of prayers, as school became a spiritual home to me.

Apart from Mass, I liked spiritual reading best. We trooped into chapel and read devotional books. There were stories of saints and martyrs, adventure stories of a high order. There were prayer and devotional books too, but also other books which aspired to make us think. I sat there and began to do theology, which was set to become an important discipline to me and, in its own way, a kind of spiritual home. This was a good place to do it: a school that was dedicated to learning and to objectivity; an environment where questions were honoured and answered and, above all, taken seriously. When the Second Vatican Council opened in 1963, the sister who taught me religious education started to lend me books which gave an account of the work of the Council. They promised a new vision of Church, of liturgy, of society. I thrived on them.

Previously my spiritual home had been supplied by my background. I was born in 1947 into a devout religious family in Edgbaston in Birmingham. My grandfather had been doctor to the priests at the Birmingham Oratory where we worshipped. His patients ranged from bargees on Birmingham's canal system to Tolkein the novelist, via Laurence Olivier who was learning his trade at the Birmingham Rep. Grand-père, as I was taught to call him, was an Irishman. I never knew him as he died just before the end of the War, so before I was born. He was one of a family of seventeen children, living proof of a birth-control-free zone. I was told that his mother enjoyed playing cards and that she would rock the cradle of the most recent child with her foot as she did so. She died on Good Friday, shaming everyone by playing bridge the day she died.

I made my First Communion at the Holy Child Jesus Convent in Edgbaston. I still have the dress, wrapped in tissue paper in an old-fashioned Harrods box, as my mother gave it to me for my fiftieth birthday present. It is beautiful, even now, with a silk under-petticoat, gauze and lace frock and a hanging pocket for my mother-of-pearl rosary. Best of all was the net veil with a cluster of artificial orange blossoms to hold it down. I stare out from my First Communion photo, back-lit, with a strange sense of destiny. I have very few memories of the actual day, but I know that I was a profound believer at the time of my First Communion. I knew how to pray and wanted to pray. During the day before the First Communion Mass, we had a retreat in the school grounds. We made little altars I remember and were encouraged to play with them, kneeling in front of them as aspirant communicants, rather than standing behind them as priests.

I loved going to the Birmingham Oratory, especially on weekdays. This was largely because it was something my mother and I did together, on our way to or from the Five Ways where we went shopping. I was allowed to ride my bike on the pavements and when we got to church I parked and went in with her to light candles and pray. Church was a friendly place, even when I lost my hair there. Aged eight, I had my first real short hair cut. My golden plaited curls were removed. My mother said that we should bring them home, so we had them put in a carrier bag. They barely fitted. On the way home we did our usual trip to the Oratory but my mother said I should not bring the bag into church. We left it outside, under the stone seats below the flags of granite which recorded the names of the members of the Oratorian community. It did nothing to protect my hair, which was duly stolen. I was aggrieved. Why should my hair have been able to go into church on my head, but not when it was in a bag? Did the Church have a problem with girls' hair?

Going back even further I read in my 'Baby Book', which my mother gave me for my fortieth birthday, that on my very first outing ever, I was taken 'Just round the corner to the Oratory in the car. Christening Day – pouring with rain and very dark and cold.' Now this was Palm Sunday, 30 March 1947. The priest was Father Denis Sheil, the final novice whom Cardinal

Newman had admitted to the Birmingham Oratory community. Father Denis had married my grandparents and my parents and baptised my brothers and sister. At my baptism the scene was set for my First Communion and all my subsequent communions. At the First Communion the tramlines were set out that would take me to St Mary's, Shaftesbury, and thence to the religious life. I was committed to a journey, catapulted from home to seek my home in God and God's will and destiny for me.

On rereading the Baby Book, I now realise that I was cast in that role from my very first Christmas. Here is my mother's account: 'She thoroughly enjoyed herself. Turkey, plum pudding and champagne for lunch and even, I believe, a sip of port. Her stocking was filled and she had lots of lovely presents. After tea when the children did the Crib Scene in the Drawing Room, Lavinia made a beautiful "Baby Jesus" and acted her part to perfection.' No wonder I look so solemn in my First Communion photo. Was I already wrestling with the doctrine of representation – about who or what can represent Jesus. Men only? Women? Children?

School at Shaftesbury, being single-sex, was pragmatic in offering solutions to such tricky questions. At Mass we had no altar boys, so a girl had to 'answer' Mass: that is to say that once you were aged over fourteen, if your Latin was good enough, you were taken off to practise 'answering'. Get it right and you sat at the front of the chapel on the left-hand side and spoke out the Latin responses. I struggled with the greatest tongue-twister of all time, the response at the end on the Offertory: '*Suscipiat Dominus sacrificium de manibus tuis, ad laudem et gloriam nominis sui, ad utilitatem quoque nostram, totiusque ecclesiae suae sanctae.*' I say these words regularly nowadays when I go to the Latin Mass at the Catholic Chaplaincy in the University of Cambridge. Sometimes as I say '*ad utilitatem quoque nostram*' – that was the killer phrase for me – I am transported back to the piano practice room at Shaftesbury where the sister who taught me English and Latin put me through my paces. I can see the little fourteen-year-old, wearing brown games shorts and a yellow Aertex blouse (why is it perpetually Saturday morning and hockey practice in my imagination?). I stand there, solidly determined to get it right, wanting, needing to be back in the manger where I played the Baby Jesus, wanting to go to a place of encounter with the incarnate God. Answering Mass would, I believed, offer me that. It might also match my huge disappointment, for I had now discovered that, because I was a girl, I was unable to aspire to be a priest.

At the time I knew that I felt profoundly disappointed. Little did I know that all the pieces were now in place for a journey that would take me on a spiritual journey of some consequence, a journey that would bring me great blessings and that would cost me dear.

2

Religious Life

So what did being a nun mean to me when I joined the convent at the age of seventeen? Was it merely a tepid substitute for priesthood? I do not believe so. At the time I was convinced of my vocation to the religious life and treasured it. I thought I was meant to be a nun. Indeed I was certain of it and rejected the possibility of marriage represented by an endearing and persistent boyfriend who proposed to me regularly through the long hot summer of 1964. We went for long walks, watched James Bond films and danced to the music of the Beatles. Yet, as I saw it, I wanted the intensity of that kind of relationship to be with God, with access to the sacraments, to the certainty of doing God's will for me and, above all, to an active life of service in the Church. I wanted to be up and running, out there and doing things for the glory of God, a kind of 'girl James Bond' on a special mission.

Yet the vocation to religious life did not come in a sudden flash. I did not hear the voice of God telling me that I stood on holy ground. There was no secret controller in the background, daring me to venture out into unknown territory. Rather my experience of a religious vocation was altogether simpler and much more natural: I had a deep inner certainty which was formed out of normal circumstances and normal relationships. I had a quiet conviction. So I wanted it and believed that God wanted it too. When it came to the actual moment when I joined the community, I even wanted the funny clothes, the black pleated skirt and white blouse and pullover I would wear as a postulant, or apprentice, trainee sister; the full habit I would wear as a novice and later as a temporary and then fully professed sister.

I knew that the community would have me trained as a teacher, that I would be sent to university and taught to the best of my capacity. Then I anticipated that I would live happily ever after, as a teacher in one of the schools that the order owned at the time. I imagined myself back on the terrace at Shaftesbury, enjoying the changing rhythms of the school year, basking in the cycle of term and holiday and days and weeks and years of fulfilment. The theological certainties that underpinned my faith also underpinned my vocation. I was cool and determined and also slightly ruthless. I had no questions; no doubts.

On one level the convent that I joined in November 1964 did resemble a garden enclosed, as calm and benign a place as the Mendip Hospital, as fun and enjoyable a place as school. It was set to be the haven which Hopkins had promised, and I rejoiced in that notion. The actual building was red-brick, Victorian or mock-Victorian in style, but elegantly built and the grounds were handsome, with large hockey pitches where we could wander. I thought they were hideous and I missed Shaftesbury terribly, because I could not see anything from my bedroom window. All that was visible were pine trees, masses of them, and they blocked the view completely. And there was a particularly raucous bird, a jay, who got angry every morning and did what I considered to be 'town-bird' impersonations in a forsythia bush outside. I hated him. For he made me realise that I had moved to suburbia and I found it rather ordinary and ugly. There were no Downs and my spirit craved the immensity they had represented for me. This was a place that would turn you in on yourself rather than help you to look outwards.

Nowadays we are terrified of sects, and of the induction processes they use to call people into membership. We have sanctions and are concerned about the human rights issues that are involved when anyone joins anything. In 1964 no such sanctions existed. The good judgment of the nuns had to come into play. By and large it did. The process of formation was something of a trial, because it involved a great deal of physical hard work, as well as the things you would expect: separation from family, the wearing of a uniform, restricted access to letters and none to telephone calls or money. All in all, the package was hard, but to a boarding-school girl, not excessively so. I took it in my stride. After all, I was being formed, not trained, and I was led to believe that the difference was significant, as indeed it was – and is. Training is easy: you jump through hoops and learn to get it right. You learn appropriate responses (I hate those words) so that you are equipped to deal with a variety of situations and are fazed by nothing. An example: a child in your care falls sick. You know where the duty log is and fill in the correct information. You call in support staff. Basically there is a procedure to ensure that you get it right.

As a young nun, I was woken by a little girl who was crying her eyes out in the middle of the night. 'Sister, Sister,' she pleaded, 'please help me. I've lost my false tooth down the loo and Mummy will be furious with me.' I had no procedure, no textbook to consult. For a brief moment I allowed myself to feel alarmed, but this was because of the notion that one of my charges, aged all of eleven, had a false tooth. So my formation stood me in excellent stead. I tucked her up in the eiderdown on top of my own bed and stamped off in an exhausted fury to search for the wretched tooth in the bowl of a vomit-filled lavatory. OK, so I found it. She went back to bed thrilled and I turned over and fell fast asleep. Nowadays I would be scared witless. After all, I had tucked the child up on my own bed. What did that count as? It seems to me that those are the reactions of the 'training' mentality, where all that matters is the mastery of the right skills and appropriate techniques. Formation is radically different. You hand yourself over; you aspire to become a new person; you want something unimaginable. And other people's children should be totally safe with you.

My fellow novices were as dedicated and as driven as I was. We liked to excel and were competitive in much of what we did, whether this was praying or getting up early in the morning or washing up endless plates and glasses and knives and forks. Our pleasures were simple and all the more enjoyable for that, because anything could be turned into a treat. We worked hard during the day, helping to service the workings of a large girls' boarding school; relaxation came in the evening with a particularly vicious game of Racing Demon. In a sense we formed each other, because we were led from the front by the young sisters in the group who gave the best example.

My own favourite has since died. She suffered for the past fifteen years from a cancer which stripped her of flesh, sometimes of energy but never of spirit. She was hugely inspirational both to me and to the other sisters who were in formation together at that time. Some people, especially those who were novices in the 1950s and have since left their convents, have written with extreme gloom about the treatment they received there as novices or young sisters. It goes without saying that such a system is open to abuse. Yet I do not want to rubbish my community or the formation I received by playing up the difficult bits. After all, I offered myself freely and I loved the companionship and friendship I met among my own contemporaries. Of course it was hard, and at times overly so, but then anything worthwhile is demanding and I did not mind the rigours at the time.

Is that why, when it came to the early 1970s, I experienced that sense of revulsion when I heard our way of life being, as I saw it, subtly discounted? 'A nun is like a garden enclosed.' Why did I feel a sense of betrayal and unreality as I heard that Jesuit priest – to my mind – dismiss the community with his pious platitude about enclosed life? Were the members of the community – whom I liked and admired – being infantilised, as though we were 'super-nannies', fine for twenty-four-hour duty in caring for other people's children, somehow barely grown-up children ourselves? With no other outlet for the fabulous formation we had received; no wider canvas on which to paint the picture of the great work God had done in choosing us for commitment and service; no song sheet from which to sing our own personal Magnificat?

The mismatch between what he was saying – and what other clerics in the Church would happily have said at the time – and my experience of these women made me want to say, 'Enough. Stop. Think what you are saying.' Were we being trivialised, as though the only space which it is safe for women to occupy is simply an extension of domestic space? The garden that lies outside the house that is our true domain and sphere of influence. What was going on? By then, eight years after I had joined the community, I did not want to be part of any such reading of the role of nuns. Dimly, if I am honest, I can see that I was just beginning to read experiences with a feminist hat on. My disenchantment with havens 'out of the swing of the sea' was complete. I wanted to be where the action was. So what had happened? What had gone 'wrong'?

On one level I was totally happy, a competent teacher, an able form mistress. I produced plays. I sang in the school choir. I led a recorder group. For fifteen years I taught children who seemed to flourish under my care; yet huge changes were going on in my consciousness as well as in the consciousness of the Church and of the community during those long and seemingly uneventful years.

For a start I had discovered that I was not a nun. Instead, technically, I was a religious sister, whereas nuns were the enclosed women who kept the great monastic Rules of Benedict, Augustine and the Carmelites. What had led me to this conclusion? The Church itself in its public teaching. The Second Vatican Council made an enormous impact on people of my generation. It turned round the way we thought about ourselves, about the Church and about God. It galvanised us and gave us a sense of energy and faith and hope which made us happy and confident in facing the future. After all, the world was in turmoil: we had seen Jackie Kennedy in a bloodstained dress, bent over her husband's body in a car in Dallas; we were watching Vietnam on our TV screens, with live body-napalming and live body-bags; we had seen Neil Armstrong walking on the moon. Our mental and emotional landscapes were changing all the time. The Council gave us the confidence to believe that the mysteries of faith were big enough for us to engage with this tortured, complicated world, as well as the benign world-to-come for which I had prayed since childhood.

The Council offered me a new self-image. As a child I had thought of myself as a vehicle, as someone in whom God's will would be wrought, as a passive recipient. Now I learnt about the vocation of all the baptised, about the sense in which every Christian was called to holiness. This was heady stuff. Suddenly, co-operating with God's will became all-important and a way of aspiring to holiness. Moreover this was not simply some kind of personal insight; it was about the self-perception of the whole group, as well as individuals. If we were not nuns, what were we and how did the contribution we could make as women religious fit into a wider whole? How could we be part of the fullness of church life?

With a changing understanding of religious life came new ways of being religious. The old model, which was largely about conformity, began to dissolve. So things like standing together before meals in order to say grace in Latin seemed suddenly to be redundant. Keeping silence for long stretches of the day also seemed less important. These were monastic practices, highly respectable customs in a way of life which was dedicated to seeking God through the observance of hours and cycles of formal prayer, but not particularly helpful to busy schoolteachers whose lives were dominated by an academic rather than a liturgical calendar. In their place we had to find a new way to live.

Now this was a genuine dilemma. Somehow we had to renew ourselves and there were no role models. Only the secular world had icons which leapt into the public imagination: Elizabeth Arden, Marilyn Monroe and so on. None of these would work for us. The only other woman who might have spoken to our condition was Mother Teresa of Calcutta and she was busy leaving the form of religious life we represented. She was off to work with the poorest of the poor and to eschew the academic formation we had prided ourselves on offering to our young nuns. Her sisters would, as it were – and I paraphrase – be all 'hands and hearts' and no 'minds and wills'. Ours were supposed to be both, or rather all four, but our intellectual and professional formation had consequences, because it taught us to think and to ask questions and, as I saw it, the Church said that these were legitimate. The Church encouraged our academic formation.

So we were caught in a dilemma. How were we to find a good and holy and healthy way to live, one which respected the gifts of individual sisters and gave proper attention to their human development and growth and yet which honoured the call to selflessness which lies at the heart of any religious vocation? To an onlooker the greatest change was in our appearance. The religious habit cloaked individuality by making everyone look the same. It was meant to keep predatory males at bay. By the mid 1970s, if anything, it had become a bit of a turn-on which made the sisters who wore it vulnerable. We had to find clothes to wear which would mirror our self-perception as adult, self-motivated women dedicated to the service of the Church. So the habit had to go. Some of the other externals vanished too, or began to crumble, as our commitment to large institutions and to working from within them got eroded. The buzz words were all about the needs of the poor, the concerns of the developing world, the North/South divide. Social justice issues invaded the tranquil domain of traditional spirituality and it became mandatory to take a stand on certain questions.

Of course this was all a lot more exciting and interesting than boring old daily routines which kept the group inward-looking and secure. At the time we thought we were fired up with zeal for God's kingdom; in fact we were busy dismantling the very form of religious life which had supported us and the Church for centuries. In a strange way we were biting the very hand that fed us; and the irony is that the Church persuaded us to undertake this task.

For the Church of my childhood was now dismantled too. In my mind the word 'church' meant the Oratory in Birmingham, all of Rome transmogrified into a single space. Or the church had been the physical location where I went to Mass, whether at school or at home in Wells. Now my understanding was transformed for, according to the teachings of the Council Fathers, the Church was the whole people of God, no longer a building, no longer a priestly caste – the ordained men – with women attending to them and facilitating their ministry in an auxiliary role. This was revolutionary, for it led the women religious in particular to examine their own place within the official structures. We were not quite lay and certainly not ordained, so we sat uncomfortably between the two, struggling to get out.

And what about God? I have said that Vatican II changed the way in which I looked at myself and the Church, but now I realise that this had profound effects on the way in which I looked at God. After all, God had been infinitely desirable, the deepest aspiration of my heart, my soul and my imagination for twenty-something years by now. So what was to happen? Despite my earlier aspirations, in no way could I pretend that God met all my needs; nor that I was not a troubled individual, aspiring to love God yet deeply aware of the flaws in my own nature. The honeymoon was over. I had a gift for working hard and a gift for making friends, but inside all of that, inside the convent experience, I was deeply lonely and craved intimacy and care. I had been very young when I joined the community and I had found friendship with older sisters who mothered me, with close friends of my own age and, through my life at university, with friends beyond the community. God was in everything I did but I desperately wanted to know more about him.

The decision to ask to study theology was a lifeline to me, though at the time I did not realise this. At the University of London I had studied French and Spanish and enjoyed my work. I went up to Queen Mary College in 1967 and began to delve into the treasures of French literature. I became a Racine addict, loving the clean lines and proportions of his plays and secretly despising the messiness of Shakespeare. The following summer, I went to Paris and wandered around the Latin Quarter inspecting the damage of the great events of May 1968. There was rubble everywhere as the paving stones had yet to be restored. I read graffiti that told me to 'watch out, as ears have walls'. Here was evidence of further growth, for this time it was not order that attracted me but disorder. I loved the sense of liberation that seemed to surround me, even though – or perhaps precisely because – it was presented in such anarchic ways.

When I returned to college in the autumn of that year, my tutor told me to read as widely as I could, so I began traipsing my way around to other sections of the university library and devoured everything I could lay my hands on: psychology, sociology, history, as well as the French literary criticism which was supposed to be my bread-and-butter reading. I was fascinated by the study of people and how they lived and what guided their choices. I was an amateur, a detective bent on getting as many answers as possible to the new questions I was asking.

In 1970 I went on to the Department of Education in Cambridge, to learn how to be a teacher. The community's commitment to education was underpinned by the excellent training it gave to the young sisters. I valued the experience of studying in Cambridge and of learning about linguistics and theories of grammar, as well as about how to teach modern languages and religious education. At the same time I began to study theology – by correspondence, initially. I revelled in it. Here I was, an aspirant theologian with the weight of the Church's learning and scholarship behind me, for what excited me most was that the Church appeared to support and encourage me. The TV brought the Pope and Rome and what the Second Vatican Council was teaching to our screens, as well as into the bookshops where I browsed and into the libraries where I read. The Council documents were translated into English, all ready for us to devour. I saw the serried ranks of bishops deliberating things which were of passionate interest to me: what the Church was like; how we should do liturgy; and, increasingly, how the religious life could be renewed; as well as how the gospel should be proclaimed to the poor. I drank it all in.

Where I most noticed the results of the Council's teaching was within the religious life itself. Things were changing daily in the self-perception of the sisters. By now our dress had altered radically, as full-length black habits were replaced by something slightly less becoming but infinitely more comfortable. We no longer had Mass in Latin; we were encouraged to change. As religious sisters, we were reminded that we had a special, indeed a unique charism. In the case of my own community, this was a bold move. For the Englishwoman who founded the group had lived at a time of transformation and change as brutal as anything we could ourselves witness in Britain through the 1970s and 1980s. If anything could help us through these troubled times, it would be a rediscovery of her original charism and a decoding of her message. Her name was Mary Ward.

When I left the community I had the opportunity to stand back from the experience of my fascination with Mary Ward. I still found her to be an extraordinary woman and one with whom I am as happy to identify while not a member of her community, as I had been when I was within it. Both as a sister and now, as an ordinary lay woman, I continue to find her inspirational. Why is this? I suppose the main reason is that she listened to the call of God at a time when the Church did not believe that God would speak directly to a woman. Somehow she found the energy to stand up to her adversaries, to those whose contrary voices tried to silence her own. She believed in the mission and ministry of women. When *The Tablet*, the Catholic weekly, asked me to write something about her, I took up my pen with real delight. This piece appeared in *The Tablet* in June 2000.

MARY WARD

Mary Ward was born in Yorkshire in 1585. These were turbulent times for the recusant Catholic community to which she belonged. Her family home sheltered two of the Gunpowder plotters, the Wright brothers, her mother's brothers. Had she married, the intention would have been for her to secure the future for some notable Catholic dynasty; for her to breed a fresh generation of little martyrs.

As she saw it, 'some other thing' was prepared for her. This insight came when she had already crossed the Channel to Flanders, to pursue an enclosed vocation as a Poor Clare, the only opening available to a devout Catholic woman at the time. St Omers buzzed with the English exile presence: there were religious of every shade and hue and amongst them the Jesuits. Mary Ward soon fell under the influence of their charism. Here was a way of life that would enable her to journey into freedom, beyond the call of parental demands about a good marriage, beyond church demands about enclosure. Here lay freedom from the two emotional and self-imposed faults that so beset the female psyche. As she herself noted: 'vain fear and inordinate love are the bane of the female sex'.

She had other things to say about women too. In 1616, for instance, she harangued her growing community of followers. An unfavourable remark had reached her, reported to her by one Thomas Sackville, a visitor from Rome. 'It is true', he reported, 'whilst they are in their first fervour; but fervour will decay and when all is said and done, they are but women.' 'I would know what you all think he meant by this speech of his "but women" and what "fervour" is,' she retorted. 'There is no such difference between men and women that women may not do great things. And I hope in God it will be seen that women in time to come will do much.'

So what were the great things Mary Ward expected of her first companions? A desire to love and serve God in joy and freedom; the ability to prize truth; an apostolic spirit. As well as opening girls' schools in Europe, they would return to the mission field in England, for there were many families who would shelter active exponents of the Gospel; many homes in which she and her sisters could give the Spiritual Exercises to devout lay people out of the glare of the public eye. They were in less danger than the missionary priests – though the Archbishop of Canterbury said of her that she was 'worse than seven Jesuits'. Praise indeed. Not all the opposition came from such friendly sources.

Like many pioneers, she knew that the clarity of her own vision put her at risk. Her wisdom was out of kilter with that which prevailed in Europe after the Council of Trent. Yet she wanted something so simple: no enclosure, government by a woman general superior according to the Constitutions of the Society of Jesus, freedom from any need to recite the Divine Office in choir. Each of these was an act of defiance as far as a besieged post-Reformation Church was concerned. Her friends were numerous but her detractors were more powerful. They had the ear of Rome and reported their concerns about the 'Galopping Gurles', as she and her followers were called: 'The English Ladies conform themselves to the ways of seculars. They are idle and talkative. They speak at meetings on spiritual matters, even in the presence of priests, and give exhortations, to which they are trained in their noviceship. They labour for the conversion of England, like priests. They want to be religious, but not monastic.'

Which was the worst crime? Working 'like priests' or 'gadding about in town and country'? We will never know. All that we can be certain of is that Mary Ward pursued her tricky vocation through thick and thin. If we, in our own times, take the existence of modern apostolic women religious for granted, then Mary Ward and her first companions must be recognised as trail blazers: women who followed a star.

She died in obscurity in 1645 and was buried at St Thomas's Church in Osbaldwick outside York, where, we are told, the vicar was 'honest enough to be bribed' to bury a Catholic. On her gravestone is written, 'To love the poore, persever in the same, Live, dye and rise with them, Was all the ayme of Mary Ward'. What was this 'same' in which she persevered so courageously? It has been interpreted in many different ways, as indeed has her life. The happiest reading is a flashback to the vision which first put her on the road to freedom, when in 1611 she heard the words, 'Take the same of the Society', and understood that to mean that she should aspire to adopt the Constitutions of the Jesuits and the spirituality of Ignatius' Spiritual Exercises.

Arguably, Mary Ward's is the first modern Catholic woman's voice. She wrestled with and wrote of things that still matter: the place of women in Church and society; the life of faith; and our access to the Divine will. Her spirit gallops on.

No wonder her life was – and is – such an inspiration to me. Here was a woman who put God's will first; a woman for whom the journey had to be a home – she had no other. I thank God that for thirty-six years, day in, day out, I shared her religious context and concern for apostolic witness within the Institute of the Blessed Virgin Mary. My own home has now changed but the journeying goes on. I believe that I journey with her still.

3

Repression or Sublimation

'Why are some verbs irregular?' I had been teaching French for fourteen years before anyone asked me that question. As a young teacher in a Mary Ward school, I liked language teaching, largely because I operated at the top end of it, with girls who were studying A-Level French literature and translations rather than the rudiments. I think Mary Ward would have approved of these schools. They aspired to academic excellence; they offered girls the very best; they took faith formation seriously. They envisaged multiple outcomes for a young woman's life, offering a spectrum of choices as broad as those that she seized. The relationship between the sisters and the children was warm and close. I loved my work and also my pupils even though, increasingly, I asked to teach more RE than French.

The religious vow of obedience is interesting. It is not about negating the human person. Rather it is about helping someone work out what is God's will for them. This does not mean obliterating them, denying them their intelligence and their own personal interests. If anything it means fostering them and helping them to flourish. What the religious life taught me and what Mary Ward in particular helped me understand is that God does not desire to crush us. Our own worst enemy lies within. 'Vain fear and inordinate love are the bane of the female sex,' Mary Ward wrote. I treasured her insight because it offered me freedom and I tried my best to build upon it and explore what it could mean for me and for the community. After all, ours were turbulent times, both in political and in church terms. Right from the very beginning of my life as a modern language teacher I had a personal secret passion, for I particularly enjoyed the works of the French playwright Racine and revelled in explaining to seventeen- and eighteen-year-olds that there was an alternative vision to the multi-faceted, chaotic one presented to them by the works of Shakespeare.

As I saw it, Racine was altogether cooler, regular, rather than irregular. His world was intense but essentially ordered; chaos came when the ordering went wrong; when passion erupted and became destructive. His plays mirrored something back to me which I found I liked and valued. For his was a world in which feelings were repressed at their peril and in which, as I saw it, they could be sublimated at will. I learnt from *Phedre* that languishing and burning could happen all at once, and that pleased me. After all, a religious vocation draws on such emotions. For love is a required virtue and the love of God is the greatest of human ideals. Anyone who languished and burned after God could surely do no wrong.

What I failed to notice was the application to my

own life, for what Racine really demonstrated was that sublimation too was as costly as repression; that it too had its shadow side; and that the hubris of my own ignorance would come back to punish me as surely as the fates and the gods punished the characters in any of his plays. The pagan world of Greek classicism, which he leant upon, plays out our evil more surely than we know. At the time though, I was cosseted spiritually and was led to believe that piety was about feeling good, rather than about being honest. We were encouraged to seek the effects of atonement, feeling saved or, as yet another Jesuit father who regularly preached to the community would insist on calling it, 'at-one-ment'. To me this meant feeling at one with God and united to God's will and purposes, rather than trying to grapple with the damaged psyche each of us bears and trying to be honest about that. The closest thing I have ever had to a mystical experience came one day after he had given us a talk. I felt that my languishing after God had been met. Yet I craved the sense of burning which the great mystics wrote of, the sense of being overwhelmed and possessed by God.

I did not know then that the only burning I was ever likely to get would be from newspaper headlines which made a word-play on my surname and from a then unknown Benedictine monastery in the States where a book I would subsequently write would be 'burnt' or otherwise destroyed.

What I now suspect is that the priest in question, with his white, podgy hands and well-laundered shirts, was somehow selling us short. He had huge influence on the community and I hate to disparage him, as he was dearly loved by a number of the sisters. I learnt later that he had been consulted when Tampax first came upon the market. Should the sisters be allowed to use them? No, he declared, in case they might be sexually stimulated by the feel of them. Such arrant ignorance of human sexuality, let alone women's bodies, still enrages me. It is a mini paradigm of a whole set of reactions which is far too familiar to far too many Catholic women. When I first heard this story I laughed from sheer disbelief. Now I feel repelled by it. As I see it we are asked to receive our wisdom from male celibates who are afraid of our bodies and baffled by the simple logistics of menstruation and female sexuality. What they do not realise is that men become the enemy when they dictate in terms like these.

The priest in question preached an emotional piety to us, rather than offering us the same kind of rigorous theological training that he, as a Jesuit Father, had enjoyed. He visited regularly; his one and only book was distributed to each of us. From it we received genuine help with prayer. Yet he taught us what I assume he considered to be a version of Christian truth that was suitable for women, because it would not tax our brains and it would feed our 'affective' lives. The Church itself, in the past, has done this too often to women for me to lay any blame at his feet. I simply notice that in my professional life I was offered the very best kind of university education; in my spiritual and affective life, I would now claim that I was not.

I learnt more from my study of French literature than I learnt from my studies as a young nun. For Racine knew about the dire consequences of repression. His plays are full of the light that floods into a Greek amphitheatre, a place where human beings acted out the drama of the human condition and did so, oddly, behind the protection of tragic masks. His imagery is all to do with what appeals to the eye, so to me he offered insight into the human condition, as opposed to a verbal commentary upon it. His use of time and place and plot gave an explosive intensity to the story-line of his plays. Racine taught me how to value clarity and order. I also think that he made me feel uncomfortably suspicious of disorder and of human passion at their most uncontrollable. He spelt out the consequences of these to maximum effect. He teased me because he kept reminding me of the importance of truthfulness.

I used to say to the girls whom I taught that Shakespeare was like making tea. His plays began at the moment when you first felt like a cuppa – or even on the far-off hillside where the tea leaves are first picked – so you stood at the sink and dreamily filled the kettle, the mud from your gardening gloves mixing with your teabag as you grubbed about dipping into the tea caddy. Then you stood about with Falstaff or Bottom or Malvolio waiting for the plot to thicken, for the dream to unravel or for the battle to begin. Eventually the kettle boils, the cauldron boils over and the full passion streams forth into a satisfying conclusion. You drink your tea.

With Racine, though, the action begins much further into the process of denouement. He situates the action at the moment just before your kettle boils, the moment when the bubbling water goes ominously quiet, the moment of implosion when human passion prepares to be revealed in all its raw intensity. One of my great hopes at the moment is to find time to reread the plays I once taught, to revel in *Andromache* and *Phèdre* and to understand the outcome of their fatal passions, as it were, for the first time. I would love to return to the raw light and clarity of Racine's work. Having said that I know I lay myself open to a charge. What about my own emotions as I began a satisfying teaching career? What did it feel like to teach other people's children and to be denied the opportunity to have my own? What about sex?

These questions are not peculiar to the religious life; many women have to live without the quality of partnership which they crave. Many women have to live without children, either because they choose to or because they have no choice. Yet the issues in question gain a particular intensity in the case of young women religious. Our life was sheltered. It was nevertheless extremely fulfilling. As I look back on it now I realise that I want to ask further questions. At the time I was very happy and I enjoyed what I was doing. Yet was my own work as a young sister and as a teacher of French language and literature about repression and denial? Was I putting sexual feelings on some kind of back burner and pretending that my own life had no emotional content, or was something else going on? Nowadays I would rephrase that question: does religious life work?

I would claim that it does and that I and my companions in the community were loving and generous people. This was sublimation, if you like, and I would argue that it is quite different from repression and somehow less toxic, unless taken to an extreme. Repression makes you feel angry and depressed. It turns you in on yourself; you stop breathing, you stop living. But sublimation of the kind we were invited to practise sets you free. Nowadays, of course, it is discredited, although it brings peace and serenity. As the great playwrights have always known, every life has emotional content. What matters is what we do with our emotions and whether we have any sense of control over them. In a word, we all repress or sublimate for we all inhabit emotional universes where we have to make choices, whatever our religious beliefs. I made a huge emotional choice at the age of seventeen along with the religious one, which was the public side of what I was doing. 'Joining a convent' was an idea that I could explain to my family and friends. The religious life gave me a vocabulary and context within which I could sublimate to my heart's content. The unravelling of this, its shadow side, the consequences of a quest for something so ideal would come later.

What did this unravelling look like? I think I came to believe that being good was more important than being truthful. Emotionally that made sense to me; I now understand that psychologically that level of sublimation or, as I would call it nowadays, deceit, plays havoc with your sense of integrity. There must be parallels in marriage and in the growth that married couples commit themselves to when they make vows in which they undertake to remain married for life. Any vocation is 90 per cent idealism, a wise sister would say later to me, and I believe that is true. It is part of the charm of the sense of calling, but will later be dismantled by the greater virtues of integrity and truth.

At the time, though, my heart was deeply contented. Our teaching and care of the children we taught was certainly very hard work but we did it in a warm and healthy atmosphere, that of single-sex girls' education. If anyone feels like sneering at that, I hope that they feel the full force of the ire of Miss Buss and Miss Beale and all the other pioneers of women's education. For they, and all who have worked within this experience, were happy to inhabit a world in which everything did not get sexualised, a world which was free of suggestiveness and innuendo, a world where frustration, if it occurred, was defused. There are other kinds of energy, after all. Everything does not have to be about sex.

The intensity with which we practised our faith and gave ourselves generously to the religious way of life somehow contained the other anxieties which people nowadays use sex to solve. Our life was deeply spiritually satisfying; it was emotionally comforting as well. The great questions we all ask, 'Am I lovable?' 'Am I acceptable?' 'Am I OK?' were somehow contained. On the one hand we were so busy that we did not have time to think about them; on the other, we believed that God was answering them with experiences of grace in prayer which drove out doubt and despair.

I had deliberately chosen not to get married; I did not want my own children. What I was given instead was a degree of autonomy many women would envy. After all, I could, as it were, go home at night and shut the door on the world. So I accept that I also did some of my most satisfying emotional work through teaching French literature and – and this is the point I want to press – I did so in a safe environment. My pupils were all girls. But I remain open to the charge: it is all very well to teach literature at one remove from the experience that the characters on the stage are dealing with. How was I dealing with my own raw emotions? What about my own passions? It was, after all – as I would later learn from Angela Tilby – a monk who invented champagne; who put that explosive kind of energy into a bottle and made it available to celibates in the process. No doubt that my imagery about boiling kettles had sexual overtones, but the tea-making analogy worked perfectly comfortably for me and the girls whom I taught. It highlighted the essential difference between French and English drama. With Racine there is no foreplay.

Then along came a boy with a question from a totally different order of reality. For in 1980 I found myself with a mixed class of eleven-year-olds and a solemn, dark-haired little boy called Robert, who was something of a star. 'Thank you so much,' he would say personally to me as he left the classroom at the end of each lesson. I loved him.

Now, I had never taught boys before. They were

little aliens from another planet and sometimes be-
haved oddly. Robert's good friend, John, for example,
had no collar bone. He used to do party tricks on the
way to PE. Dressed in a little singlet and shorts, he
would put his shoulders together across his chest as he
strode across the playground to the gym, apparently
caving in on himself. He did it to get attention and the
girls too looked on and giggled, for this was a Tarzan
display in reverse. I marvelled at his fragility, at the
sheer vulnerability of skinny little-boy neck and arms.
Something was unravelling within my psyche, for I
was dealing with a new dimension of life. Mine was set
to become a rounder world.

One day, out of the blue, came Robert's wonderful
question: 'Why are some verbs irregular?' So great
had been the confidence with which I had taught
French that I had never stopped to work out the answer
to this question for myself. We eyed each other; he sat
at the back of the classroom on the right, a tall window
behind him. His solemn little face was quite sincere.
'Verbs', I said, 'are like shoes. The ones you use most
often get worn out so you go off and borrow bits of
leather from another pair. You patch them. Like that
they get renewed and you can carry on using them. So
the verb "to be" borrows from the verb "to stand".' I
pride myself on that answer because he understood
immediately what I was trying to say. As I see it now,
I began to explain the structure and dynamics of
language to him, as opposed to teaching him words
and grammar. In my own life too I was struggling to
accept that life is much more of a patch and mend
affair than I had previously understood.

What I cannot now remember is how that incident tied in with another one that dates from the same period. Which came first, the French verbs question or the prayer for a gift? I would like to think that the family retreat weekend came first, but maybe it didn't. The story is a simple one: I was working at the Bar Convent (outside Micklegate Bar) in York, teaching during the week and doing various bits of youth work at the weekends. The parish was to go off on retreat, or rather a group of families from the parish had decided to set up a retreat weekend. Not unreasonably the parents fixed for me to come along and help take care of the younger generation, aged variously from six to sixteen. At the beginning of the weekend we were given labels on which to write our names, round cardboard discs which we pinned on our clothes to help us identify ourselves to each other. Once again this was a group in which boys and girls, men and women would work together. We were idealistic about Christian community – Catholic community, even – and wanted it to work.

By Sunday the cardboard discs were looking some-what tatty and were redundant anyway, but the priest had an idea for us. At our celebration of Mass, he suggested that we take off our discs and pray in silence for a while. Then we were to ask God for one single gift and to write the name of that gift on the back of the disc and hand it in during the offertory of the Mass. We were to cast our cares upon the Lord and see what he would do with them. At communion, when as a group we celebrated the presence of Christ in our midst as well as receiving the sacrament, it would be returned to us. This was a nice, simple, unthreatening exercise. The Mass began. I was distracted by my responsibilities, for the children and I had prepared some of the opening worship for the group. When the moment came to pray for a named gift, I did so in silence and then wrote down a word quite spontaneously. Round me people were asking for sensible things like 'peace' or 'justice' or 'happiness'. On my disc I wrote the word 'words', cast it into the offertory collection and sat back to wait for what would happen next.

St Ignatius of Loyola, in his *Spiritual Exercises*, acts on the assumption that you should not hesitate to ask God for what you most desire. Indeed he is confident that if you trust people with whom you are in any genuine kind of spiritual relationship, as I was on that summer day, they will always get to the root of their deep desires and pray for what they most need and what God most desires for them. This is all a long way away from the spirituality which has a devout communicant begin morning prayers by saying, 'Almighty and most merciful Father; we have erred and strayed from thy ways like lost sheep. We have followed too much the devices and desires of our own hearts . . .' The Book of Common Prayer is ill at ease with the idea that God might actually pursue his will in us by inviting us to know what we most deeply desire.

The exercise with badges and labels and little card discs served its purpose well. It recalled me to something which my father had told me about my French grandmother. He commended her long memory to me, saying 'the wonderful thing about Grand-mère is that she has never forgotten a single word that had ever been said to her'. Now I do not know if this was intended with deep irony. What I do recall is the sense that words and stories were some kind of treasure house and that, if you bothered to remember them, then all would be well, because you would always have a frame of reference for interpreting the present moment and present experience. By writing the word 'words' on my card disc, I was aspiring to be a communicator, to turn all the remembered words and stories into a new text, something to live for, something to live by.

I could pretend that I was on to something deeply pious, recalling the 'glorious deeds of God in my life' as though in some personal Magnificat. This is not the case; my theological interpretation of this event – as of the story about French verbs – followed later. On both occasions, I now realise, I was moving beyond the vocation to be a teacher to a different one. As a teacher, my task was to tell people about language and to interpret it to them through the study of literature; in my new vocation as a communicator, I would use language at first hand, learning to craft it into shapes and sentences, learning its inner dynamics, the way in which it changes colour and consistency. I was set to become a wordsmith. Modern language teaching had been a home to me; now I was set to journey to a new place, a new home as a communicator – a writer and broadcaster.

The change came about slowly and dawned on me with an incident which I would have done anything to avoid. At university I had been a student of a most

47

remarkable teacher of undergraduates. Her name was Ruth Morgan and she taught me medieval French. The campaigns of Charlemagne, the conventions of courtly love, the farces of medieval literature, poetry, plays, the account of the sack of Constantinople were all brought to life by an inspired linguist. Everything she taught somehow became memorable. In Cambridge her name is still a legend as she moved there in the early 1970s and became a Fellow at Girton College, where she still has many friends. Ruth died from cancer at the age of forty-two. She was deeply missed, especially by her husband and three sons. They asked me to give an address at the University Church, Great St Mary's, at her memorial service. I stood up in a pulpit for the first time in my life and delivered my carefully prepared script to the congregation with as much reverence and energy as I could. I had written a tribute to Ruth as teacher, as friend and as wife and mother. I felt unbelievably sad that she had died and still am extremely ambivalent about the fact that her memorial service should be the first occasion on which I read out my own words to a church congregation. Would that it had not been so.

Other opportunities soon followed. 'When the pupil is ready, the teacher appears' goes the old Chinese adage. I was now ready to start experimenting with the sound of my own voice and so the invitations began to come in. I found that I liked preaching and that the fact that I was only able to do it in Anglican churches or when invited by Nonconformists did not at first trouble me. Just as priestly ordination is reserved to men in the Catholic Church, so too is the ministry of the word. While women may read out the epistle in Church but not the Gospel so too, logically, they may not comment upon the Gospel. The practice of preaching is also reserved to men only.

Yet the invitations to preach now came in from outside the charmed circle of the Catholic Church. I began to discover a ministry which I could exercise only 'away' from my home base. This opened my eyes and my mind as well, because grace and the experience of grace were now mediated to me in new circumstances and in a new way. As well as the sheer fact of standing up in the pulpit and examining what the gospel taught, something else was going on. Because of my new-found sense that honesty was as important as feeling good, I actually had something to say from the pulpit. When I look back at the text of some of those sermons, I notice that I made all the mistakes that learners make – trying to put in too much material, trying to make an impact, trying to be clever. But there is evidence too of a desire to wrestle with the truth and to be more up-front about the dark side of human nature, including my own. 'Why are some verbs irregular?' Why are some, indeed most, lives irregular? In the end neither repression nor sublimation works. The religious life, as I was now discovering it, was about a journey towards a new kind of home, one where messiness had its place and truth should be given at least as much space as goodness. I was setting out again, best foot forward.

4

'At the Green Light'

Fresh impetus came with a new experience. As part of its acceptance of the teachings of the Second Vatican Council, the community adopted a practice which, until then, had been reserved to the Jesuits whose Rules and Constitutions were the inspiration of our own way of life. Ignatius of Loyola made a very wise piece of legislation. He envisaged a third year of formation which members of the community should be given some fifteen years or so into their practice of the religious life. It was called the 'Tertianship'. In 1980, therefore, I had the opportunity to take a year off teaching and to go through an intense period of further training. After nine years of classroom teaching I was excited at the prospect, as I would be doing a whole series of very different things. After all, this year of new training was to be given in an amazing variety of contexts. At first I had no idea what I would be doing, but then it gradually emerged that I would work in a hospice for six weeks, then in a youth centre, with the Afro-Caribbean community in Bayswater and at an all-night refuge near Liverpool Street station in London.

Of all the experiments, as they are called, this was my favourite. One of the homeless characters whom I met called herself 'Rita Tangerino'. She was as colourful as her name because she was a pyromaniac and specialised in throwing lighted toilet rolls through high windows. Consequently she was not allowed to carry matches, which was tricky for her as she was a heavy smoker as well. I would light her cigarettes for her and then sit on the steps of the old Victorian institution where we were stationed and listen to Rita's ramblings. I became mesmerised by her accounts of life on the street and the jagged ramblings of her freewheeling mind. Her one desire was to set something alight and soon after I left she was once more back in prison for a fire-related offence. I don't know why I liked her quite so much. On reflection I realise that she and her life were so much the antithesis of my own that in a strange way I needed her more than she needed me. This was an outcome which Ignatius knew about and for which he had prepared me. I felt elated.

These 'experiments', as Ignatius called them, were intended to be experiences that imitated the formative influences on his own life. For in the development of his own journey and life of faith, he had had to work with the sick and the needy, to travel to places and mix with people whom he might otherwise not have met and to live and learn with them. He was keen to offer the young Jesuits who first became his companions the same opportunities that had worked for him. He was interested in churning people up, in changing them and their aspirations. In my case this most certainly worked.

The most important of the experiments was the chance to make Spiritual Exercises, or month-long retreat, which he had developed and written down for others to use. I set off to St Beuno's, the Jesuit retreat house in North Wales, with a certain amount of trepidation, because I knew that my life would indeed be turned around by the experience. At the time I could not realise just how much. For going through these experiences was like opening up a Russian doll. Every time I thought I had arrived, I discovered a new shell which was to be stripped off and reconstructed. It is part of the genius of Ignatius that he gave people the opportunity to reinvent themselves. He had been given the opportunity to do just that when he was injured in a battle at a place called Pamplona in 1521. As he recovered he began to experience the call of God and to know that he was to serve the Church. Over the following years, by being attentive to his own feelings and noticing what drew and attracted him and what repelled and discomforted him, he opened up a new path for himself, for his first followers and for the Church.

So this tertianship year turned out to be a trans-formative one. When I completed it, I too began to go down this new path. The first change I noticed was that my energy for teaching began to evaporate and I was distressed by this as I had so enjoyed teaching and now it became a terrific grind. I felt guilty about my students as I had been accustomed to giving them my very best shot and now I found I could no longer do so. So very gradually I moved sidewards to a new job. This took me out of the world of secondary school education into a new one. I can write that sentence quite calmly now; at the time the experience was traumatic. After all, the community had made a huge investment of time and energy in sending me off for the tertianship year. And now, on my return, I came back with a clear sense that my teaching days were over. This led to a discrepancy between the expectations of my legitimate superiors and my own sense of God's call. I did my best to do what I was told, but became increasingly miserable.

When the next stage of the journey emerged, it moved me inexorably onwards and, to my intense relief, a new home awaited me. I joined two Jesuit friends as a colleague at the Institute of Spirituality at Heythrop College in London University. Not only was I teaching boys as well as girls, in the sense that our students were men as well as women, but I was also working with ordained and un-ordained male and female colleagues. I loved the university world and the experience of mixing with people who were far brighter than I was. I lapped it all up. We taught a subject called spirituality; that is, we sought to explain how people have lived out their beliefs down the ages. We studied the great texts from the tradition: the writings of Benedict, Ignatius, Julian of Norwich, the Rhineland mystics; we trained people in the art of spiritual direction and retreat work; and we edited two journals of spirituality. We reflected on the ways in which people nowadays search for personal meaning in their lives.

I still teach spirituality and find myself drawn inexorably back to some of the work we did at the

Institute of Spirituality at that time. The copies of *The Way* and *The Way Supplement* which have my name on the inside cover (to mark up the fact that I helped co-edit them) remain a faithful resource to me. There were three of us: two Jesuits and me. We were bright, probably ambitious, certainly energetic. So we threw ourselves into the task of making a worthwhile international project work well. I began to move in a new world where I met the academics and authors of our articles on a regular basis. I travelled to the States and to Canada to see them. I did a stint at the Jesuit retreat house at Guelph in Ontario, familiarising myself yet further with the insights of Ignatius and his Jesuit companions.

On my first trip to New York, I visited the Empire State Building and the Metropolitan Museum. I had my photo taken with King Kong and when I look at it now, I can see how happy and excited I looked. This was all a long way away from the world of Rita Tangerino, and I could easily have forgotten all about her or about the sick people whom I had helped nurse and the children whom I had taught. The valuable thing about the way of life which Ignatius invented is that it asks you not to discard your experiences but rather to fillet them, to notice them while they are going on and then to observe how you feel about them. In this way you learn what is good for you and you learn what to avoid. I have odd flashbacks: a walk on the shores of the Pacific Ocean; a visit to Castro, San Francisco's gay district, where I met a young man who was dying of AIDS and who talked with passionate intensity about the need for honesty. I can remember the thrill of seeing proper Mickey Mouse cactuses in Arizona; my first glimpse of the Grand Canyon; the green waters of Lake Louise; the Catholic Church in Montreal. My eyes were being opened, but so too was my heart.

Soon the inevitable happened: I began to write my own book. I remember the cleaners who did out our offices at seven o'clock in the morning. 'You doing overtime?' they would ask as they came in and found me pounding the living daylights out of my first word processor. I would laugh and carry on. The words kept coming and soon *Women before God* was ready to be touted around the publishing houses. At first it did not do well. I had over-reached myself, revelling in the art of writing rather than in the craft and discipline of communicating. Form won, content came second.

Eventually a break came. Judith Longman, the editorial director at SPCK, rescued me. She had found a 'reader' (someone who scrutinises a manuscript on behalf of the publishing house) who had said that she would work with me to improve the text. This she duly did. The reader's name was Angela Tilby, who was a BBC television producer at that time. I went to visit her and my ordeal began. For fortnight by fortnight, Angela plied me with ideas and attacked my writing. She taught me the use of the blue pencil or red biro. She forced me to write short sentences. She made me kill off my luvvies. As a media journalist herself (making TV documentaries for the *Everyman* series) she knew the importance of rigour. This was a lesson I needed to learn and I remain endlessly in her debt.

Those brutal editing sessions could only have produced either intense dislike or firm friendship. Rather
than longing to get the dust of her off my feet, I found
the latter, for in the event, we became good friends.
Angela shared her intelligence with me but also her
confidence that I had a gift which should be encouraged. I was able to reassure her. This was not a gift, as
I saw it, it was a grace and one which I had prayed for
fervently.

I now knew that I had received the grace of
'words', so what was I to do with it? Writing was an
obvious outlet and *Women before God* did well. I did
not know how strongly I had come to feel about the
place of women in Church and society until I wrote
that book. I wrote about my own sense of a call to
priesthood; I reflected somewhat bitterly on the idea
that I felt I was being punished for a sin or an offence
which I had not committed and which de-barred me
and other women from a place in church life to which
God might call us, but men forbad us access. In my
mind and heart I wanted everyone to be able to serve
in the Church to the fullness of their capacity. I
wanted other women to enjoy the opportunities for
travel, whether emotional or literal, that I was now
enjoying. I wanted them to be able to study and
to gain from the clarity and lucidity which, as I saw
it, the study of theology offered. I was touched by
the number of people who wrote to me when the
book was published and said, 'You have put what I
have been feeling into words.' I suspected – and I am
sure that I am right – that I had a duty to use the gift
I had been given, and that I should not write as a

private hobby but as an evangelical act.

No one has ever condemned *Women before God* or attempted to censure me for writing it; yet, in its own way, it was a seditious book as it quietly and determinedly set out the experience of being a woman in the Roman Catholic Church in ways which were bound to raise questions. It reflected a believer's world. It was directed at other women like me, as well as at the men I knew who wanted to know what it felt like being a woman within this world. My Catholic background and experience came pouring out into print.

Then another new opportunity presented itself, one which would bring me out of a world where faith or religious belief were assumed into a more public and more agnostic world, one where belief would have to be mediated quite differently. It happened quite simply. One of the producers of BBC Radio 4's *Sunday* programme came through our open-plan office at Heythrop College one day, to interview one of my colleagues at *The Way* in London. I made her a cup of coffee and asked what she did. I discovered that she was a producer for the 'Thought for the Day' slot on the *Today* Programme. I was – and am – a passionate listener to *Today*, for this is radio journalism of the highest order. I liked 'Thought' as I came to call it and asked her if she would ever consider taking on someone like me.

'Send me some trial scripts,' she said, and I duly did. A casual remark, the offer of a cup of coffee, my enthusiasm or presumption: does God really work in such overwhelmingly ordinary ways? I was to find increasingly that this was the case for I joined the 'Thought for the Day' team of presenters and, bar a couple of years' break, have remained part of it ever since.

Radio broadcasting terrified me at first. 'Thought' is transmitted live, so presenters go down to the studio and join the queue of the great and the good who line up there, awaiting their interviews. My adrenaline score would go through the roof as I got myself ready to go live on the green light. Bits of this energy rush were exciting; some were terrifying. For example, I enjoyed a game I invented. Put simply, this was a straw poll. As I walked into the *Today* hospitality suite I would always say good morning to whoever was sitting there. Some politicians were rather grand and failed to answer. I awarded them '*nul points*'; others were friendly, though as tired as I was, so we sat in comfortable silence. They got eight out of ten. Best of all though was Gary Richardson, the sports commentator. One time, as the PA (production assistant) was preparing to lead me off to the studio, he came in search of a cup of tea from the breakfast trolley in the green room. 'Enjoy your broadcast,' he called out to me and smiled.

Enjoy my broadcast. Now that was a new thought. I have never forgotten it, because of course if you enjoy what you are doing, your voice sounds quite different. For a moment I thought disloyally that I would prefer to be doing sport rather than religion. After all, there seemed to be more to enjoy in sport. I was wrong. Religious broadcasting, like religion itself, can be huge fun. After all, the news which it is supposed to communicate is meant to be good. And good in my vocabulary means energising, happy-making, simple – and fun. Now, 'Thought for the Day' is driven by news events. Only when you have read the newspapers can you speak to your producer on the telephone and negotiate a topic for the following day's broadcast. 'Thought' is always live, which means that it can catch and speak to a late-breaking story, even a tragic one. The best script I have ever heard was the one broadcast by Canon Eric James on the day after the *Marchioness* disaster, when the River Thames took a crowd of partying young people on a pleasure boat to death and disaster. Eric James' broadcast carried endless woe for us all, and especially for the bereaved. He spoke of his own experience of the river; he had authority; and he had something worthwhile to say.

I hope what I said myself on the day after fifteen children and their teacher were shot dead at Dunblane in Scotland served the same kind of purpose. When I left the studio, feeling quite shaken myself – I think we all were – I met a PA standing in tears, sobbing that she too needed to 'tell it to the bees'. This is what I had broadcast:

THOUGHT FOR THE DAY

BBC Radio 4 – 15 March 1996

When my father died, my mother sent me to tell the bees. I had to stand at the entrance to their hives and whisper the news to them. I was desolate. But this ritual helped me accept the finality of his death. And that is what ritual does so well. It helps you put into an action what you can't say in words; it helps you act out feelings you didn't even know you had.

In the aftermath of the massacre of children and their teacher at Dunblane, most of us share a sense of shock and hopelessness. You don't have to be Scottish to realise that the life of an entire community has been violated. You didn't have to be Welsh to experience the awesome force of destruction that overwhelmed the village of Aberfan in 1966. There is something particularly shattering about the mass slaughter of children. The massacre of innocence.

But what happens now is within our control. Already the enquiries and investigations are under way, and quite rightly so. The evidence must be examined, all possible leads be followed. Even though they come to the same conclusion: that a madman with a gun has done something terribly evil and wrong. To name that sin is essential. We have the right to know that evil has been done. What concerns me though is that even as we give a name to this evil, we should be careful not to seek further culprits or to attach guilt where guilt does not belong. Our desire to exonerate ourselves from blame can all too easily lead us to seek others to blame. Yet blame may not be the order of the day. After all it risks seeping into the souls of those who are left behind. 'If only I had done this', 'If only I had done that'. What is done is done. May the souls of all the departed rest in peace. And may the souls of those who are left behind be consoled and drawn to peace.

How can this be? Well, for a start, through ritual.

*We do it spontaneously. We lay flowers. We did it at
King's Cross. At Hillsborough the fans used football
scarves for the same purpose. Outside Philip Lawrence's
school, his pupils left prayers and cards. These gestures
are as old as religion itself. They have a remarkable
ability to offer healing because they do not silence grief.
Today is another day and tomorrow is but a day away.
Somehow alone or together, all of us – and not simply
the people of Dunblane – need to find time and space to
tell it to the bees. Through some small action or gesture
to put our thoughts and feelings into the hands of God.*

Does 'Thought for the Day' serve any other purpose
than to comfort the afflicted in the event of a national
tragedy? I believe it does. For a start it is not about the
presenting broadcaster's own personal or private
thought. The purpose of those two-and-three-quarter
minutes is surely to trigger off a thought in someone
else's head, namely the listeners', so that they have
something they can take forward into a busy day. After
all, it is not meant to be opinion for the day, platitude
for the day or, worse than that, wind-up for the day.
The fact that 'Thought' is presented only by people
who are practising members of the major faith communities in the United Kingdom is an attempt to
guarantee that it should not be a private platform
where a private opinion is aired. That could deteri-
orate into simple propaganda. Members of a religious
community – meaning church or synagogue or
mosque or congregation – are accountable to that
community, as well as to God, for the values they seek
to promote. They are not and must not be opinionated

mavericks, bent on getting their own way.

Does that disqualify me as a religious broadcaster? For now I am no longer a member of the community which was most closely identified with me, even though I remain a Catholic. When I first realised that I would have to leave my community, I wrote down a list of people I would need to tell. The obvious ones were the sisters in the community in the UK. Others included my parish priest. High up the list came the BBC's head of religious broadcasting, the Revd Ernest Rea. 'Does this mean I have to stop broadcasting?' I asked him. 'We have you as you,' he reassured me, 'not for the handle you have in front of your name.' I found this deeply reassuring. After all the greater community I belong to *is* the Catholic Church rather than a named religious congregation within it.

A good 'Thought', it seems to me, will reflect that sense of being part of a wider whole, of belonging to a community of faith with a given tradition. Some of my own favourites reflect what it feels like to a Sikh or a Jew or a Muslim – as well as a named kind of Christian. I like stories about rabbis or the great leader, Guru Nanak. I like the homely detail, the ability to disclose something personal without embarrassing people with gory details of one's private life. The great secret surely is to have a gift for narrative; to know which stories to tell because they give up their meaning within the right time-scale. People are not left dazzled or baffled by them. Word pictures work as well, little portraits conveyed with the right kind of adjectives so that they convey colours and sounds and graphic sketches. Nothing has so taught me to respect radio as writing scripts for 'Thought for the Day'. For at its best radio is the most intimate medium there is. It is in your home or your car. You listen at your most vulnerable, half asleep or in your night clothes, struggling to get breakfast or to prepare sandwiches for work. It goes without saying that to be part of someone's life and home and family is an immense privilege.

As I have come to realise more and more, while needing the presenter to be part of a religious denomination, 'Thought' is not beholden to the Churches or the faith communities. Much recent controversy about the place and timing and quality of religious broadcasting misses the point. No one has the right to broadcast; no one can demand to be on the radio. Someone who contributes to a programme is always there as a guest of the licence-fee payer, with all the duties that entails. That is why good broadcasters neither proselytise nor sermonise. They seem to know instinctively that they are there to 'educate, inform and entertain' (words of Lord Reith, the first Director General of the BBC). This, after all, is *broad*-casting, not narrow-casting. The sower who goes out to sow has to be generous with the seed, casting it in full confidence that the wireless is a generous medium, one which embraces and calls people in, rather than one which excludes them.

The spiritual discipline which goes with being a radio broadcaster is a very demanding one. This is the most ephemeral of media. You cast your words upon the air and have to let them go – along with your reputation, your personality, any sense of achievement. One day when I was working in Cambridge, the gas man came to call. As I led him down to the cellar he said, 'I know who you are; you're Sister Thingummy.' 'That's the one,' I said. 'I knew I'd meet you sometime,' he went on, 'seeing as how I work round here.' I value that conversation as it forms a treasured memory of how anonymous radio work is. You can walk down the street and travel on public transport while enjoying complete anonymity, unlike your colleagues in television, and nevertheless be engaged in a spiritual quest. The gas man did not need to know my name nor I his. As a member of the listening public, he was an instant ally, albeit an anonymous one.

So what is it like to become part of someone's prayer life, part of someone's spiritual journey? Very soon my contribution to radio religious broadcasting extended beyond 'Thought for the Day'. 'Prayer for the Day', which is transmitted earlier in the day and prerecorded, was an obvious extension of this work. The programme finds people at an even more vulnerable moment, when they may indeed want to pray and lack the energy for it because it is transmitted at an unearthly hour each morning. 'Prayer' is a private affair, whereas radio's principal act of public worship aspires to be much more public. I first began to broadcast the *Daily Service* on Radio 4 some eight years ago. This is the world's longest-running radio programme. In January 1998, the BBC kept its seventieth birthday and I edited a book about it at the time. It brought together a collection of scripts accompanied by prayers which listeners had sent in. These came with their comments, which in turn revealed what a faithful following the programme has. The most remarkable letter tells its own story. I loved receiving it and love reading it still.

Thank you for the Daily Service. *I look forward to listening to it every day. I live here with two ghillies, the stalker, seven dogs and an exceptionally loving Highland garron pony. Every day since I came to live here in October, the stalker and the ghillies go up the hill about 8.30 a.m. and I am left completely alone in this amazingly beautiful wilderness with my God and the animals. The nearest human being is a four-hour walk across the mountains or a twenty-minute sail by boat, so your service is my only contact with other Christians. I sing the hymns – the herons, curlews and gulls join in the prayers – and listen to the accompaniment of waterfalls, waves and wind. About 4 p.m. they all come back from the hill and about their business as I do. We seldom have time or inclination to sit and chat so most people would think that I'd be lonely – far from it, God is very real and close here. I have felt his wonderful love and care every minute of every day. Once or twice I've faced death when an unexpected gale blew up and our little boat had a wee bit of bother getting through the mountainous seas to Mallaig harbour. But the lifeboat was on standby and even though at the time we didn't know this I have no fear at all. Is it a silly thing to say that I felt cosseted by love? So thank you for the* Daily Service, *my fifteen minutes of companionship with others worshipping.*

Without feedback from listeners no one would be aware of the range and the influence of radio broadcasting. I sometimes reflect that there is a strange irony in the fact that my own Church will not let me preach because I am a woman, and yet that I am able to speak about the spiritual life to millions of listeners through the work of the BBC. I also notice that I am not allowed to lead worship in church. Yet on the airways I can use this extraordinary medium to become part of a praying community that extends far beyond these limits. I lead people in worship. I pray with them and for them. At the end of each service I call down God's blessing upon them. No wonder I am inclined to thank God for the BBC and, increasingly, the other media and production companies which enable me to proclaim the word 'in season and out of season'. Nothing makes me happier than the sight of a microphone and a radio headset. I sit down in front of it, put the cans on my head, line up my script and stopwatch, and wait for the green light to go on.

When the University of Birmingham made me an honorary Doctor of Divinity in June 1997, this vocation as a public broadcaster was recognised in a magnificent public ceremony in the University's Central Hall. I have the video of it and can see myself, a small figure with a wide smile, almost skipping up the aisle with pride and pleasure, weighed down under the ceremonial gear and the handsome floppy black hat with its golden tassel. I see my mother and brother, and kind friends who accompanied me that day. The University Orator, Professor Antony Bryer, was eloquent in his praise of 'Thought for the Day' and of my own contribution to it. My mother gave the magnificent red hood with its blue lining to me for Christmas that year. The supplier at the gown manufacturers turned out to be an avid reader of *The Tablet* and secured a beautiful secondhand gown for me to go with it. I now had the kit and the identity. Little did I know that one day I would need both. Little did I know what lay ahead of me.

5

'A Loyal Daughter of Holy Mother Church'

'Tell me then, love, what's a laity?' I sat with an exhausted team of BBC TV sound and lighting engineers, their producer Angela Tilby and presenter Francine Stock. The date was November 1992. We were in a makeshift studio above the great debating chamber where the Church of England's General Synod meets. Heavy TV cables had been hauled through the windows taking the drama enacted in the building that day out through its walls to the waiting world. For this was the day when the Church of England voted to ordain women to the priesthood. Now, at ten o'clock in the evening, everyone was tired and ready to go home. Yet there was one more interview to be filmed before that would be possible, so yet more waiting.

The debate had been passionate; the voting dignified; the result electrifying. I had been in the visitors' gallery as an observer. Now I had a more workaday role, for I had gone out to buy burgers and chips for the crew. We sat and ate them in numb silence, barely able to taste our food, exhaustion blanking out the sense of excitement the vote had engendered in us.

Then a sound engineer turned to me and said, 'Tell me then, love, what's a laity?' I looked baffled, so he added, 'You see, I usually do sport. Outside broadcasting. Football. And today they've been on and on about the House of Bishops and the House of Clergy and the House of Laity. So what is a laity?' 'Someone like you and me,' I was able to reassure him. 'A team player.' Now that was a concept he recognised. In fact it was what he had been modelling to me all day, for no TV production can dispense with team players. I looked at the massive cables which he had wired up, covering the dangerous sections with tape so that the rest of us would not trip on them. I saw them snaking their way out of doors and windows which looked as though they could not have been opened for years. I admired his physical as well as his technical skill. Without a sound engineer, we would hear no voices; without a lighting engineer, we would see no pictures. Members of a television production team have of necessity to work together and for and with each other if the final product is to be a seamless garment and to look and sound beautiful. No one can afford to be a prima donna in a world where team work is all.

I have often reflected on that moment. What indeed is a laity? Who and what are the laity? And why did Anglican women in 1992 aspire to be other than laity? A lay person is a regular believer, someone whom God calls – for it is God who gives us our vocations, we do not create these for ourselves – to live their ordinary lives as believers. A lay person is someone

69

who tries to live honestly in the real world, witnessing to the power of the gospel in a series of normal contexts which lie well away from the rarefied atmosphere of church buildings. I remembered a story I had been told. A cardinal is reputed to have said at the First Vatican Council, 'The laity, who are they?' 'And one of his colleagues answered, 'Well, you would look jolly silly without them.' The lay vocation is the vocation we all have: the call to be a loyal devout servant of the Lord. A lay person is an integral member of the body of Christ. The laity are the faithful.

How did the ordained women's vocations differ from this? I learnt the answer by listening to them. I heard extraordinary stories of a new identity which these women had discovered for themselves by listening faithfully to God's call. I liked this word as it is such an important one in the Christian imagination. For 'listen' is the word that begins Benedict's Prologue to his great Rule. The monk is to be someone who listens. That is the gift whose importance Benedict signalled up for the whole of church life, not simply for monks and nuns. In the case of the women deacons, I discovered that the call to priesthood came as much from their congregations as from anything they might have cooked up on their own. It was reinforced in their prayer and work and now the Church too was ratifying it. I recognised and valued the integrity of their sense of call because during the tertianship year I too had been reinvented. The journey is our home. Things change.

For some time I had been working with groups of

women deacons because they asked me to give retreat days for them. Often I did these with Angela Tilby as she was an Anglican herself and understood the scene better than me. We would trundle off to different parts of the country for a weekend in a retreat house and meet up with groups of stalwart women who were convinced of God's call to them. They came in all shapes and sizes; they belonged to every blend and shade of Anglicanism and what they had in common, namely a sense of vocation, was the cement that kept them together. After all, they wanted to do good, not bad. In the communities where they worked they were recognised by the laity who valued their work and wanted them to proceed to full ordination as priests. Many of their ordained male colleagues trusted and valued their work as well.

So what was God calling them to? As I saw it, they could not possibly be any kind of threat to the right ordering of ecclesiastical life because the deep desire of their hearts was to serve God within the Church. I reckoned that the Church was lucky to get them. They were bright; they were loving; they were gifted; and they were dead normal. All they aspired to do was to celebrate the gift of life which God gives to us all and which many of them, as women, had already nurtured in their own homes and workplaces. I felt privileged to be part of their training and to support them while they waited in the wings as deacons, preparing in hope for their Church to welcome them as priests.

Yet this experience was costly to me. While I enjoyed working with and for the Anglican women, something was shifting within my own consciousness.

If these women could be ordained, what about my Roman Catholic friends? What about the Catholic women whom I was meeting and who claimed that they too were experiencing God's call to priesthood? They too were dead normal, sane, bright women and clearly gifted enough to offer themselves for service in the Church. Why should they be told that they could not aspire to answer a God-given call to priesthood, simply because they were women? Even as I began to harbour these thoughts, I would repeat a formula of words over and over to myself, using it as a kind of mantra to keep myself sane. I had learnt it from a letter Mary Ward had written to the Pope when her own actions were called into question by the Church: 'I am and always have been a loyal daughter of holy mother Church.'

Yet, as I saw it, the Church was in turmoil. I would meet friends who would tell me that they had stopped going; that now their children were grown up they had had enough; that they found God in other ways and other places. The gap between many people's beliefs and the ministry of the Church was widening. Who could best bridge this gap? How could the Church be made to work once again? I know that I was not alone in asking what model of community might best answer the Church's need to be a real presence in local communities. 'What's a laity?' the sound recordist asked. What's a clergy, for that matter? What is the Church meant to be like?

I find it fascinating that it was exposure to the world of the media which made me question some of the assumptions with which I had worked most happily since my childhood and during my early years as a religious, when I thought that hierarchy was all and that mine would inevitably be an ancillary role. After all, I had bought that myth lock, stock and barrel. I thought that I existed to serve. That was what being a garden enclosed was all about. And now, through the work I was doing with and for women, my mental frame of reference was being dismantled before my very eyes. The simple question 'What is a laity?' made me think again.

When I eventually left the community, I inevitably received some hostile comments in the press, as well as some generous ones. I was intrigued to read of myself in the newspapers that I was considered to be a 'media nun'. The most forthright personal condemnation of me came from a man who wrote to tell me that 'Listening to your interview (on BBC Radio 4's *Woman's Hour*), the frequency with which you used the first person singular, made it quite obvious that what you are suffering from is an advanced case of self-adoration. This is quite common amongst those who reach "stardom" in film and other media.' I hope that I don't have self-adoration, yet it does not surprise me that this should be a charge laid against me. After all, from outside, the media world looks rather more glamorous and illusory than most. The truth of the matter is that my experience of this world did change me, not because it gave me illusions of grandeur, but because it rocked some of my theological certainties.

For I was exposed to a living and working and totally secular model of what team-playing looks and feels like. Everyone has to wait while the lighting engineers adjust their lights. No team would be complete without a sound recordist. The specialist skills of each of these players are essential to the success of the whole enterprise; a radio programme or a film or a documentary is essentially a collaborative process. As I began to do more TV work I noticed that hand-shaking is an important part of BBC culture. When you go out to a location and meet up with the crew you shake hands. You make physical contact with these people as they are the artists and craftspeople who will enable your work and your word to have some kind of flesh. When you listen to the radio or watch telly, the presenter may be the person you hear or see, but without a skilful producer and crew nothing will go well. This is team work in action and when I was first exposed to it on the green light, it left me not with *folie de grandeur* but with misgivings about the ways in which the Church can organise itself.

In November 1992 it struck me as a further irony that the sound engineer in question would otherwise be recording sport, for there too the disciplines of interdependence have to be practised. Players play for each other as well as for themselves. This was true participation, true collaboration. It put much of the Church's practice into the shade. I loved the delicate balance it represents where power gets passed around and people have to respect each other and depend upon each other and wait for each other. They also have to wait for imponderables like the sun and the clouds and the light – in the case of telly; and for aeroplanes to pass over – in the case of radio.

I so admired the world of religious broadcasting that I thought it would never bring me into conflict with the Catholic Church. To put broadcasting and religion together seemed to me to be a natural extension of the gospel command to go and teach all nations. Unfortunately, though, my writing did expose me to conflict. My first venture into print had come back in 1989. *Women before God* was a book which managed to span two worlds. First, it was intended to be a spiritual book rather than any great work of theology. So I used the telling quotation or the telling image to make my point, but mainly I talked about my own experience of growing up as a devout little Catholic child, young nun and now middle-aged woman. The letters I received from readers – men and women – were extraordinarily appreciative. Yet there were other readers too and they belonged to an increasingly vociferous group of Catholic women who were fed up and angry at the treatment handed out to them by the Church.

For the impact of Christian feminism was now being felt in all our Churches. Various debates raged: about what women could or should do in church, about how God is named in public prayer, about the relationships between ordained clergy and lay people. In a nutshell these were always questions about power. A Church like my own which centralises power in Rome and spreads it outwards in a fan shape from pope to bishop to priest somehow runs out of energy when it comes to the final gesture of devolving it upon the laity. This was part of the gripe, for the women who wrote to me felt that they were invisible and that their massive contribution to church and public life was somehow ignored.

The Second Vatican Council had empowered the laity by telling us that lay people mattered and that they counted; that the word 'vocation' both could and should be used of their state, just as much as of the religious and priests. But in the event what did this mean? How could the Church deliver while it still continued to restrict the access lay people in general and women in particular had to its power structures and to its money?

I turned increasingly to lay voices in the next writing project I undertook. For I began to edit a book of women's spiritual writings. Called *The Hidden Tradition*, it brought together writings by authors as varied as Catherine Booth, the 'mother of the Salvation Army'; Marguerite d'Oingt, a medieval Carthusian prioress, who talked of the death of Jesus on the cross as though she were a midwife watching the birth of the world; a Quaker woman, Caroline C. Graveson, who wrote, 'There is a daily round for beauty as well as for goodness, a world of flowers and books and cinemas and clothes and manners as well as of mountains and masterpieces. God is in all beauty, not only in the natural beauty of earth and sky, but in all fitness of language and rhythm.' I loved these writings as they were a faithful record of the world of 'flowers and books and cinemas and clothes' through which God talks to most of us. To talk about women's spirituality is not to enter an esoteric world of convoluted mysticism; it is to live in the ordinary world and see it as 'thin' because it is a vehicle for God's grace. There was a commonality to these writings which meant that a Catholic or a Methodist or an Anglican had more in common as women than they realised. They wrote with utter conviction about God and about the work of God in their lives. Their devotion to the person of Christ was absolute. He was the liberator who offered them more than recognition; he gave them the power to be set free.

No wonder I put Mary Ward up there with the stars, for she had written that 'vain fear and inordinate love are the bane of the female sex'. She knew about the lack of any sense of self-worth which can erode belief. 'Do these things in love and freedom', she had urged her sisters and then added, 'or do them not at all.' Her own sense of the presence of God was conveyed in a piece of writing which I put in the first chapter of the book: 'He was very near me,' she wrote, 'I saw him enter my heart.'

To discover this hidden writing, I explored libraries all over London and well beyond. I visited convents and university libraries, clambering up to dirty, dusty books which had been unopened for years. The end result was a beautiful book, as I saw it, a varied and energetic collection of authentic, original spiritual writings in which women revealed their concern with the life of faith and of grace. Until 1917, when the Congregationalists first recognised God's call to women, none of the characters in *The Hidden Tradition* could have been ordained. There were abbesses and nuns and sisters among them obviously, but their sphere of influence was no less considerable than that of the lay women, such as Margery Kempe or

Margaret Clitherow. These women were role models. That is why it seemed important to rescue them from oblivion. When I finally held the book in my hands I felt sudden pride and elation. To have edited it seemed like an important thing to do.

At the launch of *The Hidden Tradition*, Angela Tilby made a speech. Suddenly she said, 'I see a whole shelf of these books, or rather more like them.' I rose to the challenge and the following year produced a second volume to what was rapidly becoming 'the collection'. This time I turned to the missionary women and read astonishing accounts of their heroic deeds. By now I was beginning to collect books myself, so there was a double outcome: my own work but also a research tool for other women who might want to work on these texts in greater depth. While I continued to visit libraries, I also realised that there were treasures to be found in the most remote of second-hand bookshops, so I began to develop a library. By now I had left the Institute of Spirituality at Heythrop College and was working at the Council of Churches for Britain and Ireland. My brief there was to examine the place of women and men in the community of the Church, namely in all the Churches that were joined as fellow members of this ecumenical partnership. This campaigning role on behalf of women tied in perfectly with the historical project of uncovering hidden literature about the contribution of women to church life.

I became something of an expert, my nose twitching when I travelled around the country addressing various groups of women, giving retreats and quiet days, conferences and lectures. For everywhere I went, there was bound to be at least one second-hand bookshop and there I would be able to find books such as *The Gobi Desert*, the account by Mildred Cable and her companions Francesca and Evangeline French. They crossed the Gobi desert five times and penetrated into deepest Chinese Turkestan. Another firm favourite was *The White Queen of the Okoyong* by W. P. Livingstone. This told the story of Mary Slessor who took the gospel to what we now call Nigeria. Then there were the Sunday-school prizes, wonderful books with black-and-white plates and titles such as *Missionary Heroines in Many Lands* and *Missionary Heroines of Our Times*. This was literally true: the tradition which had taken women overseas in the service of the gospel was one which was still alive and well when these books were written. They formed both a commentary on what was going on and an unusual kind of heroic biography, a hagiography for our times. I loved these books and lined the walls of my office with them. They made a quaint backdrop for some of the work I did there but also offered a kind of commentary on it.

For I began to realise that these women, who thought they were going out to tell other people about the freedom intended by the gospel, in fact started receiving it themselves. Out there in the mission field they enjoyed a degree of freedom from the life of the institutional Church which meant that they could invent and improvise, using their own reactions to the situations they found, relying on their own judgment rather than the teachings of any patriarchy. Some of what they met was horrendous. Mary Slessor, for instance, found herself up against the custom of twin slaying and soon put a stop to it. When twins were born, both would be killed as one would be carrying an evil spirit and the mothers had no idea which this would be. So both had to go. In India, the missionary women were able to go into the zenanas where they took the gospel to women who lived in segregated communities as wives, and they taught them to read and write. When they met it they tackled child abuse in the form of temple prostitution. They pioneered intermediate health care; they taught hygiene. And, in the case of my own personal favourite, Gladys Aylward – the small woman, as she was called – they undid the torturous bindings with which the feet of Chinese women were deformed. In the symbolic ordering of things, the work of the missionary women had an extraordinary impact on me. I admired their courage and their bravery; I thought their faith was astonishing. I thought their imagination and reckless-ness were inspirational.

Volume three, *The Hidden Voice*, became a project that was very close to my heart. For I treasure the whole idea of education and I believe that the first educators of girls put something new into the Christian imagination. For an educated girl will have new aspirations; she will rebel against anything which curtails her freedom and trivialises her intelligence. We laugh too easily at the achievements of Frances Mary Buss and Dorothea Beale. A colleague from Miss Beale's school, namely the Cheltenham Ladies' College, wrote of her:

To Dorothea, to teach Scripture was an experience so deep and so wonderful that she longed to share it with every aspiring teacher. 'I should like most of you to look forward to Scripture teaching as a privilege to be desired', she told her staff. 'It is a sacred ministry, a sort of priesthood, this touching of sacred things, this breaking the bread of Divine knowledge for our children.'

Could these women ever be at home in the Church or, like the missionary women, would the journey also become their home, namely an internal journey to new forms of freedom, unimagined by their forebears? Some certainly came unstuck, because their attitudes put them into conflict with the male chains of authority which controlled orthodoxy. Others made the best of a bad job. They put up and shut up. For others, though, a new campaign emerged as the idea of ordination for women began to surface in their thinking. Dorothea Beale was one of many women who, unwittingly perhaps, made the spiritual connection about 'breaking the bread of divine knowledge' long before any practical or political connection had been made.

Yet this is precisely where progress was to be made for and by women. In *The Hidden Voice* I included as much political and social history as I could, demonstrating that the daughters of parsonage and manse who became suffragettes or who joined the suffrage movement, were inspired by the gospel. They saw it as their Christian duty to promote equal rights for women. They used the artefacts of their religious culture to proclaim the new gospel of liberation:

campaigning songs for hymns; coloured banners and holy pictures for inspiration; they had their saints, Millicent Fawcett and the Pankhursts, and with the death of Emily Davison, who threw herself under the King's horse at the Derby, their very own martyr.

At that time I regularly met Derek Worlock, the late Archbishop of Liverpool, at meetings and enjoyed talking with him. 'Oh, hello Lavinia,' he would say, whenever we met. And then he would add triumphantly, 'my mother was a suffragette'. I never knew whether I should say, 'Oh, I'm so sorry' or 'Oh, I'm so glad'. So instead I smiled – as he did – and told him that my grandmother had been one too. She had wanted to join the Edgbaston Ladies, a group that met in Birmingham. My grandfather forbade it as the Edgbaston Ladies had burnt down the cricket pavilion at St Philip's School, a deed which apparently put them beyond the pale. Worlock, though, promised hope. He was evidently working with the idea that there should be more lay collaboration in the Church and seemed to be totally at ease with women. His mother's training stood him in good stead.

My own training within the community was now being developed in a job that required me to think really hard about what Mary Ward had meant when she first said to the gathered sisters in St Omer in 1615 that 'it will be seen, in time to come, that women will do much'. As I travelled and visited groups of women from all our Churches, I began to realise that the past, which I had captured in the 'Hidden' books, had its contemporary counterpart. There was still work to be done to ensure that the voice of Christian women should be part of the debate and dialogue about the future of the Church. After all, as Mary Ward had taught me, 'I am and always have been a loyal daughter of holy mother Church'. Now that the 'Hidden' project was nicely rounded off with three handsome volumes to its name, I was an author in search of something to write. The opportunity was not long in coming.

The die was cast. The journey had been a slow and unspectacular one. The good little Catholic girl from the pious background had become a young sister. The young sister had moved through a variety of circumstances and experiences to a place of uncertainty about the Church and its teaching on a restricted role for women. Looking back, I cannot identify a single moment of conversion. All I know is that the Church itself, by encouraging me to read and to think, as well as to work hard and to pray, led me inexorably to work for change. It was only because I believed that what I was doing was God's work that I undertook the next stage of the journey. It is only because I believed that the Church accompanied me as well as encouraging me on this journey, that I remain its loyal daughter.

6

The Travelling Bug

For a while, though, I wrote nothing; I travelled instead, visiting Hong Kong for a ten-day conference on the work of National Councils of Churches and then venturing into China. I am so glad to have seen Nanjing and Shanghai before they were in any way 'westernised'. The contrast with Hong Kong – which I loved – was absolute. I will never forget the sound of bicycle bells and spitting as I ventured out at night and walked through the unlit streets. It astonished me that I felt so safe. Though one day I stood in Shanghai in absolute misery at a bus stop, the rain pouring down inside the collar of my yellow Chinese silk anorak, soaking the layers of my pullover and vest. I had the address of my hotel written down – in Chinese, of course – on a piece of paper, and that was all. The woman whose job it was to herd the queue onto the bus summonsed me to the front with the two ping-pong bat implements she used as signals. I grinned the widest smile possible to thank her, feeling big and awkward and clumsy beside her and the other people in the queue. Nowadays she is probably quite blasé about foreign visitors, but then I was still enough of a stranger to merit attention.

There was a grand hotel with western-style facilities at the corner of the street to which I was travelling; I stayed in the guesthouse which was built within its orbit, in a dark room which seemed to be lined with mahogany. It was like being in a coffin and I felt slightly sick, especially when I discovered cockroaches in the bathroom. I grew up a lot on that trip to China as I began to understand what a cushy life I ordinarily led, with objects of beauty all around me and no bugs to speak of. The next day I too rode a bike, lent to me by Teresa Chui, the sister whom I was visiting. She took me to her convent, explaining that I would not be able to stay there. She was Chinese and had lived and worked in Korea with sisters from my own community; then she had ministered to the Chinese community in Canada before returning to her own country, aged over seventy.

At first I was puzzled to be put in a guesthouse, but I soon understood why I could not stay in the community house with the sisters there. For the building had been taken over by the Red Guards during the 'Cultural Revolution' and treated as brutally as the sisters themselves. As Christians, as Catholics and visibly practising as such, they had been disbanded, returned to their own homes and hidden by their families. Little had been done to restore the convent building when they were able to return to it as, naturally enough, the sisters had no money. When I visited them we squelched our way over wooden planks which had been thrown down into the mud outside the front door to provide access. The door was

wide open. It was February, yet the windows too were
thrown open as the air outside was deemed to be
warmer than the air within. Either way I nearly died
of cold.

I met Teresa Chui's students, novices of the newly
constituted religious congregation which nowadays is
permitted by the state. I gave them a class in English,
describing my home parish back in London: I talked
of the notices you would see as you walked through
the church door, advertising the services, of course,
but also demonstrating the variety of things that
parishioners got up to – their good works, their social
clubs and so on. I talked about what you would see in
church and who would be there. I described the ethnic
mix and the blend of ages you would see in Kentish
Town where I worshipped on an average Sunday at
that time. They listened and asked questions. At the
end, they did something totally unexpected. They
came up and felt me, touching my face and my hands,
stroking my arm and petting me. I was baffled at first
and then I realised that I was the first sister aged forty
or thereabouts whom they had ever seen. Not only
was I white, but I was middle-aged as well. They
needed to know what I felt like.

The older sisters in their congregation dated from
before the 'Cultural Revolution'. They had gone back
to their own families during it and hidden their identity
as religious. In easier times, their Bishop had gathered
them together from a variety of former congregations
and put them into a homogenised group which would
be acceptable to the authorities. There are those who
question the validity of working 'with' the government,

which is what this 'half-and-half' or 'Patriotic' Church does. The Vatican has severed relationships with it, so that the only parts of the Catholic Church which are recognised by Rome are the truly hidden or 'underground' Church which has no truck with the state. These are difficult times for Chinese Catholics, especially for the wonderful women who joined the religious congregations some fifty years ago.

Aged seventy and above, they are guardians of a variety of traditions. I found them unbelievably brave. When I went into the chapel to pray with them, I was astonished to find that it was full of European religious artefacts, reminding them of the origins of their way of life in western culture. To the young sisters who have had no exposure to the kind of European influences which they must have experienced in their early formation, I was a bit of a freak, and also, I like to believe, a sign of hope. I thought of them when the moment came for me to sign the piece of paper which was sent to me from Rome when I asked for it and which dispensed me from my vows. I felt their hands pulling my sleeves and pinching my arm to make sure I was real and could hurt as they did and tried not to feel that I was in any way betraying them.

Some of my best memories of the visit to China have to do with food. In a restaurant, to say grace before eating was a risk – and so a necessity. It became exciting to do quite ordinary things like say your prayers or own a Bible. I visited a Bible factory and was thrilled to see copies being mass-produced and prepared for transportation all over the country. The energy and enthusiasm of the young Christians I met was extraordinary, for my colleague at the China desk of the Council of Churches for Britain and Ireland had fixed for me to visit Catholic seminarians and talk to them, as well as to students from the Protestant theological college. I ate river fish that day, caught from the local stream. On an internal flight, I was terrified when my neighbour lit a primus stove in the aisle of the plane and began a bit of private tea-brewing. At Nanjing the students each had a Thermos of hot water for making tea and they crashed about their college with these Thermoses along with their books and plastic bags. Plastic was everywhere, in troubling quantities as heaps of empty water bottles blew about in the wind and the grass when I visited the shrine to Sun Yat Sen, the founder of nationalism. Lift your eyes from the ground and the view was spellbindingly beautiful; look downwards and the debris of nascent tourism was overwhelming.

At the time, I became fascinated with all things Chinese. I devoured Jung Chang's book *Wild Swans* and then was delighted that it was shortlisted by the women's campaigning group, the Fawcett Society, for their annual book award. I had begun to attend their meetings and to be briefed by them about the social and political issues which were of increasing concern to women I met in church circles. My job enabled me to build bridges between informal as well as formal networks and to make helpful connections. So I was thrilled to be asked to be a judge of the Fawcett prize that year and to draw up the shortlist and choose the winner. A group of us were assigned this task. We read our way through a splendid collection of books and met for the odd dinner to chew over our choices. My chief memory is of the prize-giving itself, for Jenni Murray of *Woman's Hour* fame – a fellow judge – turned out to be a doughty ally and good friend of the causes I espoused. A month later, we all went off to the London School of Economics for a remarkable lecture from Jung Chang. What made it most astonishing for me was the fact that she had brought along her grandmother's little shoes. They were like dolls' shoes, some three to four inches long: living evidence of the extraordinary binding of women's feet which was practised in China in the past. Jenni Murray told me that she had already seen the little shoes in the *Woman's Hour* studio and remained haunted by them.

What about my own sense of binding? I wonder what kept me together during this period; I wonder what came to feel burdensome, because it was bigoted or unreal. These were serious questions as I had to be quite clear – in so far as one can be – about my own motivation because now I had identified myself publicly with the various causes and campaigns which placed me firmly in the ranks of the feminist sisterhood. I had espoused the cause. This meant that I too would feel I should speak out if I met injustice or unfairness. My job at the Council of Churches for Britain and Ireland gave me the ideal platform for doing this and by and large I was heard sympathetically. Of course there were people who did not like what I was saying, but I continued to accept invitations to speak in public and to try, as good-humouredly as possible, to describe what I saw.

Hard work and an identifiable sense of purpose

helped enormously at this time, as did the sense that the community liked what I did. With Mary Ward as a figurehead for our own work, it came as no surprise to anyone that a sister from the group should be doing the kind of work I was engaged in. Had I been working at the aid agency CAFOD, for example, there would have been nothing but support for what I was doing. The sense of purpose was equally important and I believed that I had the best possible reason to put time and energy into it. Many of the sisters in the group felt as I did and expressed their feelings just as clearly – if not as publicly – as I did.

Yet, was I growing out of the religious life? Was the 'garden enclosed' no more than a troubling memory, the constraints of religious life no more than irksome? I don't believe so. In London, where I lived, members of the community talked regularly of our sense of having a direct commitment to work for and on behalf of women. After all, as we met and discussed our 'mission statement' and our own sense of renewal, we had to face unpleasant facts. Whereas in China I had met a religious group that was 'bottom-heavy' with large numbers of novices and young sisters, in England – in common with many European communities – something different was going on. For our older sisters were built to last, and did, whereas some of the younger members who joined us did so briefly, or for a while, and then left.

The religious life has gone through massive demographic swings over the past forty years. There is expansion overseas: in Korea and India the novices pour in. In Europe, the States and Australia, they don't. This means that a great deal of the work which used to be done by women religious is now done by lay people. The whole project of Catholic education has been dramatically laicised. Former convent schools are now regular Catholic schools. The sisters who taught in them have long since retired and are doing remarkable work in a whole variety of different contexts. Many of them live far closer to the local community than they used to; they work in parishes and prisons and AIDS centres and homes for the care of marginalised people in ways which would have been impossible when they were running prestigious schools. There is great gain, clearly, if you take direct involvement and direct action as the main criteria for evaluating their work. Sisters do some of the most difficult and dangerous work undertaken by the Church; they often go to places where many men would be afraid to go. But there has also been loss too, because a community-based work, an apostolic project which was owned by the whole group, could carry more passengers and give a home to people of varying talents and abilities. It offered more cover, more invisibility, more time, more space. And the spirit needs these if it is to flourish.

This observation is not simply about the religious in the Church. Religion in general has far less crediblity than it did when all public works of mercy were somehow serviced by the Church. Think of a medieval town or village and the Church would have been indispensable, for as an institution it offered all the usual services that accompany birth, marriage and death; it demonstrated its commitment to the lives of ordinary people by ensuring that prayers were said for fine weather and good harvest; it provided any schooling and medical care that were available to the local community. It ran everything except the banks.

No wonder that until relatively recently the Church has expected to have a public voice that matches its commitment to human wellbeing. Yet the authority of its public voice is eroded when its values do not match those of the democratic institutions it chooses to berate. So, as outsiders see it, the Church's voice becomes intrusive and obsessed with sex. It pries into people's private lives and gives them no peace. Its passionate desire to be of service to the common good gets misconstrued and everyone loses out. A recent survey, conducted by the Tomorrow Project, gives a projected profile of Catholic Church attendance in the UK for the year 2005; the figures make disheartening reading to those who are committed to public service on behalf of the Church. In 2000, 3,814,000 people go to church, i.e. some 10.2 per cent of the population. It is predicted that in 2005, 2,825,000 people will go to church in the whole of the UK, namely 7 per cent of the population. The Catholic totals go like this: in 2000 there are 1,601,000 people at Sunday Mass, in 2005, there will be 890,000. A diminishing flock is of necessity a poorer flock. It is likely to be an elderly one as well.

These statistics are chilling. They reinforce the sense that our common culture has gone through a seismic shift and any idea that Christianity and its culture are normative is hopelessly out of date. Not only do people not know the gospel stories; they do not care that they do not know them. In certain instances they are actively relieved that this is the case. As they feel free of an institution which, as they see it, has failed in its charge to bring life to the world, they come out of the woodwork and condemn it because it seems to them to have brought persecution, oppression and outright war. The track record is a sorry one and many church leaders despair. Yet belief in God means that people like me should choose not to feel gloomy and that we should work for change, both within and outside the body of the Church. This means more than saying prayers and teaching other people how to pray; it means walking the extra mile with the poor and needy, as well as with the rich and powerful.

Is it significant that the more political and social my own concerns became, the less I felt attracted to purely spiritual ministries and to retreat work? I found that retreat work in particular exhausted me, as it made demands that I was ill-equipped to meet. I wanted to teach spirituality; I wanted to help people to pray; I wanted to proclaim the word – in season and out of season if necessary. Yet one-to-one spiritual direction began to tire me out. I went on a lecture tour to Australia and was energised by the enthusiasm of the sisters there, yet exhausted too. By the end of my time there I was beginning to hear the tiredness in my voice. All I wanted to do was to lie on the ground and recover. When I eventually got to Sydney I burst into tears and slept like a log. My hosts were extraordinarily kind and have renewed their invitation to me to go back and spend more time with them. I make polite excuses, fearing now that my lecturing and campaigning days are over too.

A different trip, to the Philippines, the following year, was less draining, for I only had to give one public lecture. The visit was organised by a North American agency and it was about pornography and how the Churches should respond to it. The Salvation Army and American Roman Catholic Church were our sponsors. I met with Cardinal Bernadin and was heartened to think that the Archdiocese of Chicago was in such wise hands. He warmed to the topic and spoke earnestly of the need to do something to empower women in the Church so that they could take the agenda of pornography out of the hands of the professionals and decide themselves how they would like to see their bodies represented.

One of the projects I visited in the Philippines was at Olongapo, the former Subic Bay base of the American fleet. Here child pornography flourishes as there are many mixed-race children, Amer-Indian, Afro-Indian and so on. They are ravishingly beautiful and this is their downfall, as sex tourism flourishes and they have become its target.

I went to a courtroom with Father Shay Cullen, the Irish Columban priest who has been active on behalf of these children at the PREDA Centre which he runs for their rehabilitation. Two little lads sat in front of me in neatly pressed jeans. It took me a moment to understand that these were the alleged victims of the horrendous crime which had been enacted against them. They looked too small, too frail. The man who was on trial for abusing them stood nervously in the courtroom doorway, smoking. He wore black jeans and a black tee-shirt. He was a former French Foreign Legionnaire and had boasted openly to two under-cover newspaper journalists of his ability to kill. Then the judge appeared, dashed through the preliminaries and let him off, despite the children's accounts of his brutality to them. There was no case, we were told, as the children were minors. They were brothers, aged about six and eight, small boys with thin little necks that bent heartbreakingly away from contact with the adult world as they left the courtroom and any kind of justice.

I met other, happier children when I went with the Council of Churches on a trip to the Caribbean, visiting Barbados, Guyana, Surinam and Trinidad. This too was a formative experience that was easily as important as the tertianship year. My work for and on behalf of women risked making me think that there was only one area of human experience that really counted, whereas in the Caribbean I was reminded of the effects of racism on a whole economy as well as culture. I lost my heart to Surinam where the capital, Paramaribo, is like Amsterdam, without the canals. It is also incredibly run down so that when you pass small shops you make nothing of them. I needed a watch battery and went into one of these shops. It turned out to be like Aladdin's cave, full of delicate jewellery made from gold. I bought a pair of earrings, shaped like flowers.

In Trinidad I danced during the Carnival with little handicapped children from the orphanage where I was staying. We had a whole stand of seats to ourselves, the gift of some rich benefactor, and the children had a perfect day. Their capacity for enjoying themselves made an even greater impact on me than the wonderful costumes and the pounding music of the procession. I could feel the rhythm of the steel band deep inside my chest and knew that the Carnival would go on all night. It duly did.

When I got back to England I began writing again. It seemed to be the only thing which I could do to keep evil like that I had seen in Olongapo and in the poverty of the Caribbean at bay. Within two years I compiled two major collections of prayers, reflections and readings. One, called *A Time to Receive*, was commissioned by the Religious Programmes department of the BBC for use during Lent 1997. The other, called *The Dome of Heaven*, was intended to help people pray their way through Advent in 1999. It had prayers and exercises for us up to the feast of the Epiphany 2000.

I enjoyed writing these because they enabled me to reflect more on the politicised world I had walked in on, the world where I was associated with the concerns of women, and to get some spiritual refreshment for myself as well as for other people. In *A Time to Receive*, I found myself reflecting on the short version of the Lord's Prayer given in Luke's Gospel. This prayer has more immediacy than the fuller, familiar version in Matthew's Gospel and it formed the heart of the book. I have used it regularly to pray with ever since, enjoying its total simplicity.

Father,
hallowed be your name.
Your kingdom come.
Give us each day our daily bread.
And forgive us our sins,
for we ourselves forgive
everyone indebted to us.
And do not bring us to the time of trial.

Luke 11:2–4

This prayer seemed to me to offer hope both for individuals and for groups to pray together during Lent. By means of the radio I too could use it to pray with others as well as using it myself. I found that various threads of my life came together at this time. Here was an opportunity to teach people; here was an opportunity to deepen my relationship with the audience who listened to the *Daily Service*, for the readings in the book were also selected for use on the radio day by day through Lent that year. Then came a great personal thrill. For I was asked to present the *Daily Service* each Monday during this period. The producer, Philip Billson, had a really imaginative idea. We would go to six different venues, all of which meant something important to me. I was delighted.

This meant going on a journey backwards in time and revisiting some of my earlier homes. Not surprisingly I began at Wells in Somerset, where the girl choristers supplied our music. Walking over the Cathedral Green to record the service I thought of the many ironies which now enabled me, as a Catholic, to present this broadcast. As a child I had no access to the world represented by the cathedral; as an adult, through the good offices of the BBC, I was able to ask the girls to do their very best for the listeners. One of them put up her hand just as we were preparing for transmission: 'Shall we put on our cassocks?' she asked. I answered too quickly I now believe. 'No,' I said. 'This is radio.' What I now realise is that she was acknowledging that this strange medium, with all its heavy cables and microphones blocking the cathedral aisle, was nevertheless genuine worship, despite the absence of a visible congregation. Before the service began we prayed for all those who would be listening to it, especially the sick and bedridden, those for whom the children's voices would be like a breath of spring.

The following week we went to St Mary's School, Shaftesbury, and then to St Mary's School, Ascot, where I had been a young nun. To go back to each of these venues as a broadcaster was somehow to try to interpret their place in my life. So I went on to Wales for the fourth programme and revisited the Jesuit house at Tremerchion where Gerard Manley Hopkins had studied as a young man and where I had made the thirty-day retreat in the 1980s. I had first been there during a long and dark November; now I was back in the springtime, full of hope and confident that the threads were all coming together.

When the news that I had left the IBVM eventually broke in the press in January 2000, my former retreat director, Gerard W. Hughes SJ (the author of the religious bestseller, *God of Surprises)* wrote to me to remind me of that time.

*So sorry to hear of what you have been suffering from
Rome, sorry for you and sorry for IBVM U.K.*

Later he added a further note to me:

*After dropping you a line I have a flashback from c. 20
years ago when I was giving you a retreat and offered
you de Mello's statue exercise* (Anthony de Mello
was an Indian Jesuit, whose work was also subsequently condemned by the Congregation for the
Doctrine of the Faith).

*Memory can play false, but my memory of your
account of your first attempt was of your seeing a
completely bare room – no statue. The room had a
wooden floor and in the spaces between the planks little
beetles began to crawl out. Then a large pair of boots
appeared, squashing the emerging beetles. If my recollec-
tion is true, what a prophetic image it was! Your second
attempt to do the statue exercise was of you sitting in a
field of wild flowers in the sun and sipping a glass of
wine. I hope that also proves prophetic.*

I treasure both those letters and the fact that Gerry
Hughes remembered the images that flooded into my
imagination during that retreat, for it was a time of
great change for me. I felt as though I was embracing
the core of the gospel for the first time and was
determined to live out its insights. No wonder North
Wales was on the map when I did my *Daily Service*
spiritual pilgrimage.

The next stop was the parish church where I worshipped in London. A short distance from the

community house in which I was living at the time, it was also the ideal venue for my fiftieth birthday party which I celebrated that day. My community gave warm and generous hospitality to a crowd of friends when we trooped down from a Mass which was celebrated after the *Daily Service*. I felt richly blessed as now, not simply different strands of my life, but also different people from it all gathered together under one roof to party together. That Lent in general and now my birthday in particular felt like the 'Time to Receive' of the book's title.

The final service for my spiritual journey came from Great St Mary's Church in Cambridge, where I had preached at Ruth Morgan's memorial service. My life had come full circle and I remember ending the service with a special blessing, for now Lent was coming to an end. We were preparing for Holy Week and for whatever would happen next:

Keep us in peace O Christ our God, under the protection of your holy and venerable cross; save us from our enemies, visible and invisible, and count us worthy to glorify you with thanksgiving, with the Father and the Holy Spirit, now and forever, world without end, Amen.

My long-haul travels were at an end, I thought; certainly the mini-pilgrimage with the *Daily Service* was over; so my personal journey of reconciliation with the past was complete. I looked forward confidently to the next fifty years, and anticipated that they would be as interesting as the past. Meanwhile, unbeknownst to

me, things were hotting up in Rome, for my identity
as a writer was to become more firmly tied to the
destiny of another book, also commissioned from me,
a book which I had written in 1992–93 in total good
faith, yet which brought me notoriety and ultimately
condemnation. It was called *Woman at the Altar.*

I remember the moment when I was first asked to
write it. I remember the foot work I had to do to get it
right. I remember the letters of recognition and thanks
which came to me after it was published. And then I
remember the conflict it inspired. Now, in retrospect,
I count the cost. Was it worth it? My answer is a
resounding 'Yes'. As I would later say to Cardinal
Hume, it was a 'book of the moment', commissioned
at a time when the ordination of Roman Catholic
women as priests was openly discussed in the UK.

What made *Woman at the Altar* different from the
other books about women's ordination that were in
circulation at that time was the fact that I used
'Catholic' arguments in it. It seemed to me that the
theological and pastoral framework for ordaining
women was already in place. I knew women who
talked openly about their sense of calling to priesthood. Their ordination would be the logical conclusion
of all the recent work the Church had done to teach
about the holiness of all the baptised. In this sense it
would not be an aberration from the truth but rather a
fulfilment of it. If anything, not to ordain women
would be to compromise the Catholicity of the
Church. I pointed out that 'The Pontifical Commission, when questioned on this matter by Paul VI,
answered that, in their opinion, there was no valid

biblical basis for opposing the ordination of women to the priesthood.' I chose the image which was used on the front of the book with great care. It shows Mary the mother of Jesus at prayer, standing with her arms raised in blessing. Decked out in blue and gold and wearing a stole, she is dressed for all the world to see her as a priest. The mosaic in question came from the Archiepiscopal Chapel in Ravenna and made a memorable book jacket. I was proud of the book and glad I had written it, not because I considered it to be great literature, but because I believed it to be an honest account of the arguments used on both sides of the debate and so a professional piece of work.

7

A Threat too far

I could have been forgiven for thinking that my life and work for the service of the Church now had a permanent green light over it. Yet this was not the case. The first inkling that all was not well came in a letter from Francisco Javier Errazuriz, Cardinal Ossa, Secretary to the Vatican Congregation which is responsible for the care of religious and the religious life. Addressed to the General Superior of the IBVM, it was dated 21 June 1995, over a year after the publication of *Woman at the Altar*, over two years after I had begun to write it. His letter threw a shadow over my life that began as a shade of amber and would end up bright red. He wrote:

> Recently Sr Lavinia Byrne, IBVM, of your Institute, has published a book entitled Woman at the Altar. This book advocates the ordination of women as priests in the Catholic Church, a position which is counter to the teaching of Ordinatio Sacerdotalis, the Apostolic Letter issued by our Holy Father, Pope John Paul II, on 24 May 1994.
>
> Though the volume contains the text of the Apostolic

*Letter as an appendix and though there is an explan-
atory note on p. 9 which explains that her text was
written before publication of the Apostolic Letter, the
author proposes her thesis with no recognition of the
authority of our Holy Father's pontifical magisterium,
and she expresses no acceptance of that magisterium.*

This is an important letter because it lays out quite
clearly what was to be my central problem with the
Vatican's intervention. Cardinal Ossa's letter begins
with the word 'recently'. No date, no attempt to
establish a time frame, so no recognition of the fact
that the debate about the ordination of women had
been open at the time when I wrote the book. Clearly
I would be wrong-footed if it were not recognised that
I wrote the book to a tight publishing schedule,
completed it at least six months before the publication
of the Pope's Apostolic Letter, and that it was set to go
to press before May 1994. I have found it quite
extraordinarily difficult to hold on to my sense of
integrity and fairness because of this basic misunder-
standing.

Then comes the assertion that I expressed no acceptance of the magisterium. Why then did I bother to go
to the trouble of ensuring that the Pope's Letter was
inserted as an appendix to the book, so as to secure
the 'last word' for his teaching? Printing schedules in
the secular world are tight. I was pushing things by
asking to have the text included and by having this act
recognised in a footnote at the end of the introduction.
This is when my heart began to sink, for I started to
see that there is a huge disparity between the way in

which wheels and cogs turn over in Rome and the way in which modern printing presses and modern minds operate outside that particular closed world. I began to feel sick with dread.

Cardinal Ossa went on to make an important point:

Further she states, 'I also write quite deliberately as a Roman Catholic woman and a religious sister' p. 2.

Your permission, as Superior General, was required for publication of this work (according to Canon Law). *This Congregation wishes to know whether you gave your permission for publishing this text. Additionally, this Congregation would be grateful to know your judgment about the thesis advocated by Sr Lavinia.*

At the time I thought this was brutal; I still do. After all, I had written the book, not her. If anyone needed to be 'spoken to' or questioned, it was me not her. She did not need to be put on the line. She had done nothing wrong. So there is no way that the sister in question could do anything but defend the orthodoxy of the Vatican position and, as it were, capitulate. The work of other members of the Institute was far more important than mine. The community was expanding in the former Soviet Union; our sisters in Hungary and Romania and the Czech Republic were coming out of hiding and needed all the support the community and the Vatican could give them; we had Korean sisters in Macao who were busy learning Chinese so that they would be able to go into China should opportunity arise. I could visualise the consternation at the IBVM headquarters in Rome where, whatever sympathy other members of the community might have for the ordination of women, the good of the whole group was inevitably an overriding principle.

I recognise and understand and accept – though I have not seen the correspondence – that to keep the community in good standing with the Vatican, the IBVM General Superior had to write back and say that her judgment was sound, namely that it followed the teaching of the Apostolic Letter of 24 May 1994 and that she could not support the idea of ordaining women to the priesthood. I do not blame her or reproach her for this. She acted for the good of the whole membership of the IBVM and all the sisters who were in her charge. She acted in total good faith. What more can you want? Moreover she wrote to me to check out the facts, wanting to know if I had submitted the book to the requisite levels of censorship. I was able to assure her that I had.

But an icicle had entered a sensitive place in my heart, and increasingly it entered my soul. No one had taken the trouble to check out the time frame with me and to take it seriously. Cardinal Ossa's letter was objective in every particular except in its use of the word 'recently'. He ended it with good will:

We would be grateful for a reply at your earliest convenience. Be sure of our faithful prayer for you and the members of your institute. May the Lord bless you richly!

As a baby with my sister, Elisabeth, and my brothers,
Maurice (centre) and Philippe, 1947.

Aged three.   Aged four.

Recording the *Daily Service* at Emmanuel Church, Didsbury, 1997.

On the day I was awarded the honorary degree of Doctor of Divinity by the University of Birmingham, 1997.

Posing as 'Cybernun' for a *Daily Telegraph* feature, 1998.

At Machu Pichu, Peru, 1999.

I wonder if that blessing extended to me. In retrospect I now realise that there was an inherent problem with this letter and with the others that were to follow. None of them was written to me. Instead they were directed at the General Superior of the community. So what, you might say, after all she was my legitimate religious superior and I had taken a vow of obedience. No one could contest that fact. The truth is more delicate than that. For within any community there is a legitimate chain of trust. It works in both directions: the leaders have to assume good will on the part of those whom they lead and vice versa. In his *Spiritual Exercises* Ignatius of Loyola described it like this:

> *To assure better cooperation between the one who is giving the Exercises and the exercitant, and more beneficial results for both, it is necessary to suppose that every good Christian is more ready to put a good interpretation on another's statement than to condemn it as false. If an orthodox construction cannot be put on a proposition, the one who made it should be asked how he understands it. If he is in error, he should be corrected with all kindness. If this does not suffice, all appropriate means should be used to bring him to a correct interpretation, and so defend the proposition from error.*
>
> *Spiritual Exercises,* para. 22

Ignatius describes a process. He presupposes a conversation between two players who address each other directly. Neither is to claim the moral high ground; each is to listen to the other. Indeed the authority figure – the person who is giving the Exercises – has to listen, for the person making them (the exercitant) is asked to explain things and to seek enlightenment. Any correction is to be offered kindly. Flesh that out and what does it mean?

In July that year, I remember sitting on a wooden bench overlooking the playing fields of one of our former schools with a sister who was 'high up' in the community. She was visiting the UK from Rome and I was grateful to talk to her. We shared a common interest in cooking and, on a previous visit to England, she had got hold of some interesting spices and we had concocted wicked curries together, gasping for breath as we heated them up and sent ourselves into red-hot orbit, preparing private meals which no one else would eat. As we talked on that July evening, remembering the real circumstances of my life, chatting about the moments of fun like that, as well as what we both most cared about, namely the work of the sisters around the world, I felt confident in my relationship with the community.

That was a balmy, landmark evening. Whatever the shadow cast on me by letters from Rome, I was not being treated as a 'bad person' by the IBVM and that comforted me. I remember that July evening as a precious moment. I felt understood and respected. My concern with the mission of the Church and the spread of the gospel was recognised. I cared deeply about the work of the community and knew that in many respects the future was rocky. After all, our sisters in the former Soviet block were deeply wounded by the experience of communism, just like the sisters I had met in China. The Romanians and Hungarians had inherent problems and did not like each other; the Czechs and Slovaks too did not necessarily get on. Behind every so-called theological or political agenda, there lies a human agenda, a racial or tribal or – as I was now discovering – a gender agenda, a rift or fault line which seems to defy our very best efforts to heal it.

As the sun set over the hockey field in front of us, spilling its light onto the soft red bricks of the former convent buildings behind us, I would like to think that I heard the hidden voices of all the children I had ever taught; that I could see them chatting and laughing and playing as I sat there thinking about my own past, my own future and about the aspirations which the sisters had inspired in these girls. I cannot disassociate myself from this scene. I am there as a child. I can see myself charging up and down, an enthusiastic centre-half, cheered on by the school and the community, wearing a hockey badge which made my brothers laugh because it said 'Vice-Captain'; energised because my faith and my life came together and made me happy and free; glad to know that there would be doughnuts for tea and that we could play another game as we ate them, trying not to lick our lips or noses, as the sugar and the sweetness of the moment clung to us.

I am there as a teacher too, encouraging other little girls to be like me, glad to have been so well educated by the IBVM and to have inherited the charism which I believed Mary Ward gave to us: the gift of love and freedom and confidence and trust. As the sun went down that evening, I experienced clarity and hope. I wonder now, though, if that conversation did not mark the beginning of the end. I had always enjoyed that kind of relationship within the IBVM. I trusted the people who had legitimate authority over me and liked them. I was a good vice-captain, without any great ambitious desires to run the show, so a good team player, someone who wanted to hold the centre ground and make things happen in the Lord's service. Yet that was to be one of the last conversations I was to have in which I was treated as a respected equal, rather than a character in the dock, having to defend myself from charges which mystified me or which I believed to be unjust.

It was as though something was about to be skewed because a different model of authority was coming into play. After all a religious congregation is not some faceless bureaucracy; it is what it claims to be, namely a community of people who are gathered together quite randomly and who consent to work together with and for each other because they believe that God has called them to share in a common task. A television interviewer later questioned me and used the analogy of a large corporate or business enterprise when speaking about the Church. Why was I so surprised to be treated as though I had to justify myself? I explained to him as patiently as I could that the Church, by aspiring to be the body of Christ, rather than Orthodoxy Enterprises Inc. or Hell Fire plc, actually sets up totally different expectations in its members. Charity is the oil that gives it unction and life, not efficient and ruthless management systems.

I thought I stood on firm ground initially for I was able to demonstrate that I had always taken care to work within the system of internal censorship which was required by my community. No one in his or her right mind would ever write a book and submit it for publication without passing it around and having it carefully scrutinised by suitably qualified people. My earlier experience with readers had been entirely benign and beneficial even. In the case of *Woman at the Altar*, I was not writing for a religious or a Catholic publishing house; I was not seeking the modern equivalent of an *imprimatur*. I was able to reassure the relevant authorities that I had indeed had the book read and that I had jumped through the right hoops. In fact I had gone further than that.

After all, the book was about a very particular issue: the ordination of women to the priesthood in the Roman Catholic Church. I knew it was contentious and probably more so than most people did, for I had sat through innumerable debates and discussions about this very question. I knew about the blood, sweat and tears. I knew about the genuine anxiety of the opposition, about people who were concerned about catholicity or about the access women should have to the sanctuary. I knew about frail male egos as well as wounded female ones. So I consulted widely both about what I wrote and before I wrote. I read widely as there is a great deal of literature available about this subject. Yet much of it is available only in academic dress and, as I saw it, my task was to simplify and clarify the arguments by writing a book which would have journalistic rather than great theological merit. It was a 'book of the moment'.

So what was that moment? Nowadays it is hard to recall that in the UK at least, the question of the ordination of women became a matter of open and public debate in the weeks and months following the Church of England's vote in November 1992. Ordained women began to appear on our streets, wearing black clerical clothes as well as a variety of more colourful ones. One of my favourite Anglican women was a brilliant dressmaker and I marvelled at her ability to transform the stereotype by looking extremely elegant and pleasing. She would go on to do remarkable work with the most hardened of criminals in a long-term security unit. I could tell a thousand stories like hers. After all I had been conducting retreats for Anglican women deacons for three or four years by this stage and I was also very well aware of how powerful their vocation stories were. God was clearly calling women to priesthood, both in the Church of England and beyond. Women in the Free Churches who had been ordained for years added their voices to those of the campaigners and, emotionally as it were, linked arms with their sisters at the Catholic end of the tradition. I remember a diminutive Methodist minister who joined the crowd outside Bristol Cathedral when the first Anglican women were ordained and carried a banner promising support for their ministry.

Something was happening in the public imagination too and the media began to reflect it back to us. We saw the first ordinations on our TV screens; we witnessed the first Eucharists. For once the Church was providing a media story which actually edified people and made the Church seem plausible and credible. Even the tabloids carried the story. In media terms these were a series of 'good news' stories and they served to cheer people up.

The feelings they generated were a long way away from the everyday 'batty vicar' or 'child-abusing priest' stories which ordinarily make the headlines. I felt proud to be a Catholic and to be involved, albeit from the sidelines, as we celebrated something which made sense to the public and which brought credit to the wider Church. The BBC's *Vicar of Dibley*, a TV comedy series with Dawn French starring as a well-endowed rural female pastor, would take a while to colonise our television screens but the tracks were laid for her emergence. BBC Radio 4's *The Archers* too would do sterling work to demonstrate how satisfactory the ministry of an ordained woman can be. A friend told me that when she walked through the market in Norwich as a woman deacon, the stall-holders would call out to her, 'Morning, Vicar!' I admired and somehow envied her that access to ministry. For the first women to be ordained were not attention-seeking or self-publicists. They wanted to do an honest day's work in the Lord's vineyard. They wanted to get on with God's work. In them I recognised the spirit of Mary Ward who also wanted something new for the Church and the opportunity for women to go out into the market place of life and proclaim the word of God simply by being there. The fact that this required sacramental expression came as no surprise to me.

After all, as she had said, 'Women in time to come will do much.' I find myself repeating that phrase over and over. It is as though she knew that the new way of life she initiated could have only one logical outcome. The way of life she developed took the doctrine of the incarnation so seriously that no one should be surprised that it would eventually seek some kind of sacramental expression. An incarnate Lord inevitably becomes a sacramental one because we seek ways to keep his presence alive in our midst.

In 1993 and early 1994 certain Anglican priests left their Church and became Catholics; some Catholic women moved in the opposite direction in order to train for ordination (though of course this fact was not reported in the press); within time some of the Anglican priests were to move back again to the Church of their first calling. More people would follow in both directions. The Churches reconfigured and the dust began to settle.

Then in May 1994 the Pope issued a piece of papal teaching called *Ordinatio Sacerdotalis.* Its English title is 'On reserving priestly ordination to men only'. *Woman at the Altar* had already gone to the typesetters, yet, as I have said, the publishers, Mowbray, were very considerate when I telephoned them to tell them of my dilemma. For in *Ordinatio Sacerdotalis*, the Pope made it plain that the subject of women's ordination should not be talked about or dreamt of or discussed in the Catholic Church. This put me on the spot but Mowbray agreed to a neat solution. We would publish the full text of the papal teaching at the end of the book.

114

And so the book went to press. Its North American co-producers at St John's Liturgical Press in Collegeville, Minnesota, were not a secular firm like Mowbray, so, on one level, they were not free to publish such a wide range of titles. Yet – and it is important to remember this – they agreed to the deal, and the book saw the light of day simultaneously in the USA. The reviewers were generous. Letters flooded in from grateful readers, many of whom – though not all – were members of other Churches.

When Cardinal Ossa's letter was copied to me in June 1995, I had time to reflect and think. I needed to examine my conscience, to ask myself why I had written the book. Was I an honest broker, the journalist I professed to be, or was I simply a trouble-maker, a stirrer? Was I no longer a loyal daughter of holy mother Church? I gradually came to see that I was dealing with three separate agendas. One was spiritual; it was about my own conscience. One was about the community, the network of relationships which had supported me and my vocation. The final one was political; it was about me and the Church and the future.

My conscience had taken a hammering, for I felt spiritually wounded as though I was being accused of disloyalty or disobedience. Yet I was the only Catholic in the country to have assisted at and witnessed each stage of the debate within the Church of England. I had been at the General Synod meeting as a guest and felt honoured to have been there. I was in the public gallery at the House of Commons when the subject was brought to Parliament for deliberation. And I was also at the House of Lords when the legislation was finally carried. A Roman Catholic bishop was also in the public gallery on that occasion. He had to be reprimanded by an officer of the House as he was attempting to take notes during the debate and this is forbidden. I watched the back of his neck redden as his piece of paper was confiscated. I had heard every scrap of evidence within a thoroughly democratic setting. Yet being so close to the action was only half the story.

It was the retreat work with the women in question that finally convinced me that God was calling women to ordination. This was a call with a context and I had seen how that context came into being through the work I had done on the 'Hidden' project. I had seen how the call to priesthood emerged inevitably with the emancipation and enfranchisement of women for work in the public domain. The domestic sphere was no longer to be the only place where women would work. As Maude Royden had seen in 1916, change was inevitable:

Deacons, choristers, churchwardens, acolytes, servers and thurifers, even the takers-up of the collection, are almost exclusively men. If at any time not one male person can be found to collect, the priest does it himself, or, after a long and anxious pause, some woman, more unsexed than the rest, steps forward to perform this office. In one church, I am told, it was the custom for collectors to take the collection up to the sanctuary rails, till the war compelled women to take the place of men, when they were directed to wait at the chancel steps. In another it was proposed to elect a woman churchwarden, when the vicar vehemently protested on the ground that this would be a 'slur on the parish'. In another, the impossibility of getting any male youth to ring the sanctus-bell induced a lady to offer her services. After anxious thought the priest accepted her offer 'because the rope hung down behind a curtain, so no one would see her'.

Maude Royden,
Women and the Church of England, 1916

Behind the bitter irony the argument is clear. With the coming of the First World War, something changed in the human psyche. Women came out from behind the many curtains which had been erected around them. It became inevitable that in church too they would seek a new role. No wonder I could use a prophetic quotation on the title page of *Woman at the Altar*: 'God, through his daughters here is taking aim' (Thomas Blackburn).

So I could experience nothing but joy as I found myself in Bristol Cathedral when the first ordinations took place, and at a First Mass the following morning. There would be problems, obviously, for sexism is alive and well and living in the Church of England as well as elsewhere. In some places Maude Royden's unfortunate parody is still re-enacted. But for one brief moment I witnessed a real sense of achievement and of arrival. The stories began to flood in: hospital chaplaincy teams where the Catholic priest arrived with a bottle of champagne for his newly ordained Anglican woman colleague; women-only liturgical celebrations among Catholic feminists; the formation of an organisation called Catholic Women's Ordination; the emergence of BASIC (Brothers and Sisters in Christ), an Irish group which would develop a powerful website.

I knew that I was not alone in what I was thinking, that other people too shared my opinions and that they were actively campaigning for change. My conscience was clear because I knew that I was not a maverick and that I had written the book in good faith. Yet I felt deeply misunderstood and that there was no mechanism for me to communicate this fact to the people at the Congregation for Religious Life in Rome. Somehow they seemed like an impenetrable fortress, self-referring and isolated from the reality of church life 'on the ground'.

The truth of the matter is that my experience at work gave me privileged access to the debate about women and ordination. At the Council of Churches for Britain and Ireland, I was employed to show concern for the place of women in Church and society. I met people each day who expected me to carry some kind of torch for them. I enjoyed my work and found that I was supported by the IBVM community. I knew that many of the other sisters – and at the highest levels – shared my opinions. They read my books and shared my enthusiasm for the cause. Yet when I was asked to keep silent about my opinions by not speaking about the question of ordination in public, I agreed to do so. After all, I had written the book. Anyone who wanted to know the arguments had only to read it.

As I saw it there were other battles to fight on other

fronts – about inclusive language, for instance, about the money which women church workers should be paid and their terms of employment, about representation, and a host of other issues which were pressing for attention. I got on with the rest of my life, confident that the ghosts stirred up by Cardinal Ossa's letter could be laid to rest; confident that the IBVM were forward-looking and concerned to promote the concerns of women through our work in general, as well as mine in particular. About the Church I did not know how confident to be. I knew that I wanted everything to be well and to continue with the work I was doing. So, as I say, I began to refuse requests to speak in public and to avoid any situations in which I thought I might be asked to comment on the ordination of women. I kept my half of the deal, confident that I had not set out to do anything wrong and that I had the support of the people I most valued. Above all, judging by the welcome afforded to the other newly ordained women priests, God really was at work in this matter.

The Congregation for the Doctrine of the Faith

Then came the fateful summer of 1998, some four years later. An indication that all was not well with my relationship with the hierarchy came in another letter from Rome. It revealed that the book's American co-publishing house, St John's Liturgical Press, Collegeville, Minnesota, had been instructed to destroy the 1,300 copies of *Woman at the Altar* which they held in stock on the direct orders of their diocesan bishop, John F. Kinney of St Cloud. I reeled from shock.

The new letter was written by Cardinal Bertone of the Congregation for the Doctrine of the Faith on 18 April 1998. Once again it was not addressed to me but to the General Superior of the IBVM in Rome.

This Congregation wishes to inform you that The Liturgical Press of St John's Abbey has recently agreed to discontinue the sale of this book.

This action, undertaken by St John's Abbey, resolves the problem of the continued distribution of Woman at the Altar. *At the same time, however, this Dicastery asks you to inform Sister Lavinia Byrne that it will be necessary for her to correct the errors which have been disseminated by her book, by making some form of public assent to the specific teaching of the magisterial documents* Humanae Vitae *and* Ordinatio Sacerdotalis.

To say that the pace was hotting up sounds like some ghastly pun. Yet the fact that the book had been removed from sale gave me a rush of energy. Like a mother hen, I felt defensive of it. After all, it was not an evil book and did not merit such harsh treatment. Moreover the text of the Pope's Letter was included in it so, strangely, by suppressing my text they were also failing to distribute his. I felt terribly confused about all of this and only gradually did the jig-saw pieces inside my mind fall into place. It seemed to me that there were certain basic misunderstandings and these gradually became more evident to me. First, I take the fact that the American publishers had agreed to withdraw the book. They did not communicate this information to me; they have never offered any compensation to my community for the loss of earnings on the contract they had made to publish and distribute the book. They never wrote to me to explain what they had done or why they had done it.

Then there was the inherent confusion which seemed to suggest that by destroying copies in the States, the Vatican authorities were actually taking it out of circulation, so that the 'problem' of its distribution would be resolved. Surely Cardinal Bertone was misguided to believe that the book would no longer be available. After all the principal publishers were Mowbray in the UK. They continued to sell the book, ensured its distribution in America through an alternative outlet, and made it available to the increasing number of 'dot.coms' that were selling books on the Internet. Ironically by seeking to destroy the book, Cardinal Bertone gave it a certain degree of notoriety. The sales figures say it all: by 25 January 2000, 8,668 copies of *Woman at the Altar* had been sold and Mowbray, now part of the Continuum International Publishing Group, were set to make it more widely available. That day I did an Internet search for the book and found that it was being sold through eleven websites, let alone through all of Continuum's outlets in the UK, the States and far beyond.

Meanwhile I tried to find out what had really happened at St John's Liturgical Press. If they would not contact me, I would have to telephone them. In July 1998 I spoke to the marketing manager who told me that the book had been warehoused. He sounded alarmed and defensive when I asked for an explanation. A week later a Catholic journalist from the *Catholic Herald*, who telephoned the monastery for further news, was told that the book had been burnt. By now I did not know who to believe. Then, when I was feeling nothing but distress, the *Sunday Times* journalist John Cornwell entered the fray. He wrote to me and invited me to call on him in his book-lined study at Jesus College, Cambridge. This I duly did and found, for what felt like the first time, someone who asked me what I was feeling. I blurted out a totally unexpected answer. 'Bullied,' I said. He wrote a piece called 'Burnt Offerings' and the newspaper featured a full-page photograph of the book surrounded by flames. Cornwell pointed out that the Congregation for the Doctrine of the Faith is the department of the Vatican which was formerly known as the Inquisition. 'The Vatican has opened its archive on the Inquisition,' he wrote. 'But how can it hope to wipe the slate clean when secret investigations continue, and Catholics are being censored, sacked, bullied and humiliated?'

I felt extraordinarily supported by that and other articles which professional Catholic journalists wrote. They sounded sane and reasonable and they signed what they wrote so that they were accountable for it. I wondered who had written the letter which appeared over Cardinal Bertone's name, because a Catholic priest who knows the set-up in Rome well informed me that most likely the letter had been written by some junior official who was seeking to make his mark. Most likely it had been sent as part of a strategy to secure preferment for some rising star within the Vatican department in question. But now I was feeling panicky and this feeling of panic increased when the headline writers had a field day with offerings like 'Nobody expects the Inquisition' as they reported what was happening to me. Basically the sense of being 'censored, sacked, bullied and humiliated' began to erode my self-confidence. In public I would continue to function fairly normally but in private I cried and cried and ended up feeling a complete wreck.

Help came from two important sources. One was

the local parish church where I went for help and support. I sat and talked at length with the parish priest and then I asked if I might receive the Sacrament of the Sick. He went off to look for his oils and then sat me down and took me through this rite very carefully and kindly. I felt greatly comforted and marvelled that my gut instinct to turn to the Church and its sacramental system at this time had been the right one.

Afterwards we went out to the local pub and ate some dreadfully unhealthy lunch. This moment became an important turning point. For I was forced to acknowledge that the whole business was making me physically and mentally sick. The pressure was intolerable and I would have to find a way of dealing with it. The obvious solution was to go to the doctor for help and I am fortunate in belonging to one of those multi-disciplinary surgeries where help is available on a variety of fronts. Here at last was someone I could talk to and a medical pathway to lead me out of the political jungle I seemed to have entered.

Now that the story was in the public domain I began to receive letters from supporters. These were an extraordinary cross-section of documents and when I began to feel slightly less depressed and tearful, I was very touched and pleased to get them. Some put me in a quandary, like the e-mail from the American college librarian who wrote to say that she was wondering how to deal with the copy of *Woman at the Altar* on her library shelves. Students who approved of the book might steal it as a treasured souvenir; students who disapproved might destroy it as a ghastly piece of deviant propaganda. Either way she was going to be wrong-footed. Complete strangers wrote to say that they never bought religious books but on this occasion they had gone out of their way to acquire a copy. Journalists from the secular press began contacting me and their photographers lined me up for lengthy sessions. All of this gave me an opportunity to explain the situation as plainly as I could, but the damage had been done.

To destroy a book by fire or by pulping it or warehousing it is surely to use the methods of the Inquisition. If it had been burnt, then the imagery and symbolism were overwhelming, for fire in the Catholic tradition is associated with the flames of hell and carries horrendous overtones. No wonder I felt gutted. I could not believe what was going on and began to realise that I was in greater trouble than I thought. The community was put on the defensive and I think that it would probably be fair to say that, in certain cases, their support – which had been considerable – began to wear thin. No one likes to be bullied by hostile behaviour, because it introduces tension and trauma into even the best of relationships, and ours began to suffer.

So the real political agenda began to emerge. I had believed that the factual evidence about how and above all *when* the book was written and subsequently published gave me a certain objectivity. After all, it had allowed me to redeem the integrity of my ideas while aspiring to hold on to loyalty to the IBVM's official position. I had accepted silence. I had refrained from making any direct comments about the ordination of women in public; I had written nothing further about it.

So why did Cardinal Bertone want me to go public, as it were, 'by making some form of public assent to the specific teaching of the magisterial documents *Humanae Vitae* and *Ordinatio Sacerdotalis*', and what did this mean? When the media discovered that the book had been destroyed on the orders of the Congregation for the Doctrine of the Faith, the publicity was considerable. I do not think that this is what he meant or intended because, inevitably, it turned into the kind of news story which does the Vatican no credit. It cast him and his colleagues in a bad light.

Did he know that I was a religious broadcaster? Is that what the words 'public assent' refer to? In retrospect I think there is a real mismatch of understanding between church people and media people. I was one of the former but I was a sufficiently experienced broadcaster to know my way round the world of the latter. The agenda of the media is not set by the Churches and religious people are naïve if they think it is. There is no way in which anyone at the BBC would be interested in a story of submission. Ditto the press. For the media sees itself as standing over and against (where necessary) the major institutions of public life. Journalists are biased of course, but they are inclined to be open about their prejudices and they pride themselves for being concerned about the truth – as opposed to any definition of the truth which is presently in circulation. No one has the right to broadcast; no one can ring the BBC and demand airtime. If Cardinal Bertone thought that I could monopolise the airwaves with a statement which would in effect have been dragged out of me, then he was wrong. I remembered a chance remark from John Humphrys as I was on my way out of the *Today* studio after a broadcast. 'I hope God pays you well, Lavinia,' he said. 'After all, you work hard enough for him.' I laughed and left. That is the kind of image of religious broadcasting with which I would prefer to be associated.

So what did 'some form of public declaration of assent' really mean? And what was I being asked to give my assent to? Imagine various scenarios. Had I been asked to declare my faith in the key doctrines of Christianity – the incarnation, the virgin birth, the death and resurrection of Jesus – then a public document already existed and I used it every Sunday in any case. For, Sunday by Sunday, I prayed with the words of the creed and stood up in church and recited it with full confidence. I have always loved the creed and find it a profound source of theological and spiritual comfort to this day. I love the sonorous phrases and sometimes sing it in Latin inside my head, for that is how I first learnt it and first grew to realise that I would never fully understand what it meant, but that this is part of its merit. For it attempts to put the ineffable into words and is not afraid of its task. 'Set me as a seal upon your heart', I had read in the Song of Songs and I believed that the Nicene Creed is just such a seal.

For the creed is about what is central to our faith. It is a document with a history and represents the wisdom of western Christendom at its most sophisticated and refined. I would be proud to say the creed in public; in fact I am proud to do so. At about this time a good friend of mine was received into the Catholic Church. I attended the service and acted as her sponsor. I placed my hand on her shoulder as she stood up in front of the community and read out the words a new Catholic is expected to say on these occasions: 'I believe everything the Catholic Church teaches to be revealed by God.' As she said them I thought to myself, well, that's OK, and experienced immediate peace. I could say those words quite comfortably because the claim of divine revelation is one which the Church does not use lightly, and a creed is about as close as you could get to the core of our faith.

In the event though, it was not the creed which was required of me. It was assent to the 'specific teaching of the magisterial documents *Humanae Vitae* and *Ordinatio Sacerdotalis*' which the CDF was after. Everything inside me baulked at this proposal and this is why I had begun to feel so ill. To attempt to reduce the heartbeat of Catholic teaching to two pieces of recent papal teaching both of which are indirectly about women and, what a surprise, about sex, seemed to me to trivialise the whole experience of faith. I refused to co-operate. Never at any point did I even entertain the idea of agreeing to this demand. This was not a rational choice worked out by marshalling the arguments on both sides. It was a clear imperative inside my being. That sounds pompous but is the nearest I can get to saying that my conscience kicked in at this point and I could not do otherwise. I can see that this made for a logistical nightmare for the sisters in my community who were charged with the task of delivering the goods, as it were, by having me assent. Once again the chain of trust which sustains the religious life was put under threat. In its place came a blanket call to obedience, rather than a sensitive call to discernment. I was to write a letter of consent. I would not, and found it difficult to explain that I could not.

Later, when Cardinal Hume – who was Cardinal Archbishop of Westminster at the time and so the leader of the Roman Catholic Church in England and Wales – learnt that I had been put under pressure to conform, he was adamant in his response. 'Thank God you did not do that, Lavinia,' he said. 'It is the thin edge of the wedge. They'll be trying to get us all to do it soon.'

Despite the encouragement I would receive from the Cardinal's brave words I was now in open conflict with the Church and increasingly becoming a problem to the community. In public I continued to smile and to get on with my broadcasting and writing. I had moved to Cambridge by now and was teaching in the Cambridge Theological Federation. A staff member at Westcott House, the Anglican Theological College, I was training future women and men priests and ministers for service in all our Churches. Cardinal Hume knew that I did this work and encouraged me in my desire to offer theological education. I was writing hard as well and sent him copies of the series of little books I wrote on the lives of the saints. He was particularly glad to get one on St Benedict who was one of the saints I had chosen to write about. I knew that Father Michael Seed, his ecumenical advisor, had given him copies of the Lent book, *A Time to Receive*, and that he had spoken warmly of it.

So when he eventually heard that the CDF were on my trail he asked to see me. The interview took place in a room in an IBVM convent and was attended by one of the sisters in the UK who had had to bear most of the responsibility for feeding Rome's decisions to me. She had been on the receiving end of each of the letters that came from Rome and there were many of them. She had done her best but was, I believe, mightily relieved that the Cardinal was prepared to offer us time and attention. He was wearing a black soutane with red piping and little red buttons, lots of them. I found myself riveted by the symbols of his authority and was completely unafraid of this and of the power he represented. I experienced him as totally benign as he unscrambled the messy storyline, read the press release I had prepared and got me to give my own account of what had been going on. I asked him if I was now so discredited that I should never aspire to teach or work in a Catholic institution. He was adamant that the thought should not enter my head. 'This is about justice, Lavinia,' he said, 'not about obedience.' I left the room on cloud nine, my spirits lifted, and I was grateful to receive the apologies of the sister who had accompanied me to this meeting. She too was generous in the extreme.

As a result of our interview Basil Hume wrote directly to Cardinal Bertone and ensured that a copy of the letter was sent to me. Along with my receiving the Sacrament of the Sick, our interview was the first true act of kindness that I experienced from the

Church. He was intelligent enough to accept that the timing of writing and of publication put me in the clear. While not pretending that he agreed with the contents of the book or the arguments I advanced, he nevertheless defended my right to have written it at that time. My spirits lifted.

His letter to Cardinal Bertone in Rome is dated 18 September 1998.

Your Excellency
On Monday September the 14th, I met with Sister Lavinia Byrne IBVM and her Provincial, Sr Cecilia Goodman.

The purpose of our meeting was to discuss the after-math of the publication of Sister Lavinia's book, Woman at the Altar. *I explained to the two sisters that I had no mandate to interfere in the affairs of their religious Institute. I also said that whereas I had to make certain that the teaching of the Church was known and accepted by the Catholics of England and Wales, at the same time I had to ensure that no harm would come to the Church. I, too, had to be concerned that every individual be treated with justice and charity.*

Having considered the present matter carefully, having spoken with Sister Lavinia and her Superior, taking also into account the sensitivities of people in our country and abroad, I have concluded that I must advise, and strongly, that no further action be taken by the Congregation in the matter of Sister Lavinia's book.

You will recall how Sister Lavinia had explained that her book, Woman at the Altar *was completed and with the publisher when the Holy Father issued his document entitled* Ordinatio Sacerdotalis. *It was Sister Lavinia who insisted that* Ordinatio Sacerdotalis *should be printed at the end of her book, even though this caused the publisher considerable inconvenience.*

I have read Sister Lavinia's press release of 1 August 1998 and this confirmed my view that no further action should be taken. Sister wrote:

'Woman at the Altar *was a book of that moment. There is no way in which I or any other theologian could write it nowadays. I have not spoken in public or lectured about the question of priestly ordination since I was asked not to do so by my legitimate superiors in the Institute of the Blessed Virgin Mary in July 1995. I should add that I believe and profess all that the holy Catholic Church teaches and proclaims to be revealed by God.*

This statement was given publicity in the press.

Sister Lavinia is a much respected person in this country, and not only in the Catholic Church. She has done much good, and will continue to do so.

I am sure the Congregation will act wisely and with prudence, and now leave the matter to rest. Any other policy will be harmful for the Church in this country.

Please accept my advice.

I cannot describe the sense of relief I experienced when I received this letter. It was as though a heavy metal bar had been taken off the back of my neck. I wrote to thank the Cardinal for I recognised in Basil Hume the qualities which Ignatius of Loyola had identified for me in his *Spiritual Exercises*. Here at last was a church official who was prepared to hear my account of events and who did not attempt to dismiss me out of hand. He restored something important to me because he reinstated my sense of self and of mission or calling. He reminded me that the work I did was important and, like John Humphrys with his witty aside about hoping that God pays well, was kind enough to recognise that I did it as generously as possible.

More importantly than that, he eased relations with various sisters in the community who had taken sides over the question of my loyalty to the Church. When the first missives began to fly between Rome and the IBVM headquarters in the UK, I had been told, 'We cannot support you; we have to support the Vatican.' This is chilling stuff and it does deep damage. Only gradually would I discover just how deep. The real tragedy is that the pressure which the Congregation for the Doctrine of the Faith exerted on the community inevitably had this as its outcome. That is why, when I was asked what I felt about this reaction, I spoke of feeling bullied. So I would be the first to claim that what the Cardinal did by intervening was to help to sort out what was going on and to make some kind of reconciliation possible. He was a true bridge-builder.

When I next met him, at a public reception at Archbishop's House in Westminster, he went out of his way to speak to me again, telling me that I should feel peaceful and get on with my work. The occasion was an important one, a reception to attract attention to the Margaret Beaufort Institute of Theology which is part of the Cambridge Theological Federation. This

The Journey is My Home

is a project which is close to my heart, because it provides a centre where women – mainly Roman Catholic – can study theology in Cambridge and enjoy access to the same courses which are on offer to students from the other Churches who are training for ordained ministry there. The Margaret Beaufort students can do undergraduate degrees through the University of Cambridge's Divinity Faculty and also master's degrees with a range of other universities. I teach students from the Margaret Beaufort Institute and love having them in my classes. I know how important their education is to them and that they make a significant contribution to the life of the Cambridge Theological Federation. The fact that the Cardinal endorsed the Institute so thoroughly that evening demonstrated something I felt I already knew: that he was not afraid of the idea of theologically educated lay women and religious; that he knew that women's theological education had been neglected by the Church and that they have a stunning contribution to make. He gave a powerful speech and reinforced what he was saying by inviting people to give generously to the cause. 'Think of a number, double it and then add a nought,' he said playfully.

What none knew that evening as he stood looking resplendent in his full Cardinal's red was that within a year he would be dead from cancer. I was grateful to be able to make some small return to him by contributing to a book about him and by writing reviews of his final book and a collection of his public writings. My own gratitude to him is immeasurable. At a time of genuine trial in my life he restored my confidence in the due processes of law. I think his letter to the Congregation for the Doctrine of the Faith is masterly for it states the case with calm objectivity and brought about some resolution.

The fact that Rome fell silent is surely evidence that his words worked.

9

'Tell Out My Soul'

There was another character lurking in the wings. Cardinal Hume was not the only source of support or objectivity in my life. Enter the Internet, stage right. In the blue corner, I faced the Vatican, or rather the Congregation for the Doctrine of the Faith lining me up to make a public statement of assent. In the red corner, meanwhile, stood the Internet, not yet an institution but certainly a tool that was equally as powerful as the Church, yet with a totally different agenda.

I had discovered the Internet some two years earlier while at the University of North London. I went there for a year in 1997 to study information management or what used to be called Library Studies. The IBVM had worked extensively on a mission statement which committed our sisters in the UK to a variety of ministries. Mine had been identified as a media and writing apostolate and it was now recognised that I needed further training. As a community, we had gone through an extensive process of renewal which I can honestly describe as one of the high spots of my time as a religious. Organisationally speaking it helped us to examine our work and evaluate it. One of the common areas of concern was the world of communications. After all, most of us were trained teachers; we used words well and were accustomed to standing up in front of large groups of children or young adults and giving them our best.

Communication held no fears for us, so what were we doing to improve our use of the media? After all we used them extensively for we were consumers obviously, and enjoyed radio and TV, or telephoning each other and sending faxes galore. Video was also becoming part of our world. Increasingly, too, sisters were using word processors and learning to love the clean efficient world of the personal computer.

But what about our use of the media for the work we did: for trying to say something about the love of God and the value of spiritual truths and practices in the outer world? Clearly we were not planning to go down the Mother Angelica and the American Divine Word route, namely to aspire to own the means of producing TV or radio or film, but we knew that they were important.

As an indirect consequence of this general audit of our work, I had the opportunity to talk with my superiors in the UK about how this ministry might be renewed and expanded. What if a member of the province were geared up to understand more about the new media? I had a year to run at the Council of Churches for Britain and Ireland but nevertheless gave up the work I had been doing there. Any kind of campaigning work is exhausting and in reality I looked forward to a change. I was also putting myself out of danger too, because if I became involved in communications and the media, perhaps I could escape leading questions about the ordination of women which I was no longer free to answer. So off I went to the campus in North London to begin to study once again. It was a fascinating year, for I had the opportunity to learn more about a subject which had always intrigued me.

As a young teacher of French way back at the beginning of my time in secondary education, I had built a computer. That is to say that I had put together a very primitive and simple system for retrieving information. With bits of cardboard, a hole-puncher and a knitting needle, I was able to sort out my teaching resources, and I had masses of these as I was so keen on what I was doing. The early 1970s had seen an explosion of interest in audio-visual work. The very first words of Spanish I remember learning were 'Two beers and an ice cream, please', when the appropriate picture was flashed before my eyes. So I developed a repertoire of cassettes and postcards and posters, and then needed the best possible retrieval system for getting hold of the right ones in a hurry as I slid out of the mid-morning break and got ready for my next lessons. I liked the technical side of this project, enjoyed sorting out the categories I should use and devising the technological solution I needed. But best of all I liked the fact that this early interest in information management provided me with theological insights which grew over the years.

When I began university work again they were ripe for further reflection. I began to realise that any systems we make, whether to manage information or traffic flow or time, somehow copy something inside our heads. We carry within ourselves a mechanism which can help us impose order where apparently there is none. Structure is integral to human living; it is not an add-on, an impossible burden imposing constraints from the outside. I became convinced that to be made 'in the divine image and likeness' is to carry the capacity to mirror the order and orderliness which exists within God. A well-managed and system-ised way of looking after information turns it around. Arbitrary, ill-organised archives mean nothing and cannot deliver up their secrets, whereas well-organ-ised information is a resource for everyone. Now this, if you like, was a return to the ideas that first attracted me to Racine, but I had got to grips with the idea of disorder or chaos by now. I was not simply trying to build a perfect universe, a shiny-bright system where everything would look good but somehow be suspended in unreality.

To say that I became interested in systems sounds frightening at first, as though I am advocating some narrow kind of structured existence which would regiment and restrict people and move them around like pieces on a chess board. If anything I was more interested in process, in how you gather and obtain information, how you check and verify it, in what makes systems work, in what enables them to deliver interesting and truthful information with least hassle. That meant that I would need to learn about being much more flexible about human disorder, including my own, than I had been as a 'young nun'.

The reason why I go on to make a theological claim

is because I now see that part of the pattern which I perceive within God is much more chaotic than we ordinarily let on. It has the energy of the dance about it and is captured in a myriad modern ways. I became fascinated with images like those brought to us by the Hubble telescope. These were unobtainable when I was younger; they had no equivalent in the ordered world in which I lived, the series of enclosed gardens that were offered to me. Yet God is energetic and a source of energy for us and I saw that mirrored when I was given a colour photograph from Hubble. If God is as dynamic as that then surely this means that we can share some of the power of the divine life and be energised by it. To help this to happen, we have, as it were, to join the dance of God, to let God's ways of organising reality change our ways of ordering reality. My preoccupation with systems was not some poor, sad, rather sick hobby; it became a motif in my life.

I remembered that when I was a child I was hopeless at biology. So I had to do a subject at O level called 'Human Biology and Hygiene', a kind of plodder's equivalent to the real thing. I remember the row I got into when, during our mocks, an exam question asked me to describe the human skeleton. 'Without the human skeleton,' my answer began, 'the human body would be a pile of flesh lying on the floor.' It is a horrible image, a revolting one and I think I used it to scare myself rather than to wind up the teacher. Perhaps I should have said that with the human skeleton, the human person is able to dance, to eat, to make love, to engage with the supple systems of God, to become a living and organic system as well as a person and part of a universe which dances to the designs and will of God.

Not surprisingly, because I met precisely this kind of ordering in its workings, I fell in love with the Internet immediately. Just as word processing enabled me to write neatly with a minimum of crossing out, so the Internet would prove to be a sinewy friend, stretched across the world, inviting me to learn new information and to join in something grander and more magnificent as a human project than any number of libraries full of books. At university the courses I followed were about media and cultural studies as well as about systems and managing information so I was able to contextualise the net within a wider frame of reference. I learnt about words like 'currency' and 'authority'. Put simply they mean, 'How up-to-date is this piece of information?' And 'Where does it come from?' In the world of information management, these words carry weight because they help the searcher – as I had now become – to evaluate how a given piece of information fits into a wider whole.

This was not a world that revelled in censorship or which sought to punish deviancy. Within the kind of information systems I was learning about, everything would get stored, even material which did not fit because it recorded unorthodox views. Obviously any librarian can 'lose' material down the back of a shelf, but then the entire archive suffers because the voices of dissent are stifled and parts of history are consigned to silence.

Each of the students in my year had to get work experience. At the end of the December term, we vanished off to university libraries, and company and law firms. The theory we had absorbed had to be put into practice. For my six-week placement I went to the House of Commons library and was plunged into a thoroughly secular version of a culture I knew extremely well, namely the world of a large institution. I became intrigued by the idea that badly managed information stagnates. It sits tight doing nothing, whereas if it is managed well, it begins to flow. It becomes useful to all the players who need to get hold of it. Some of the jobs I did were rather menial, but while I did them I had time to think. Methodically I sorted the out-of-date periodicals so that they could be removed in coffins to underground storage. The more recent copies could then breathe and could be taken down easily to be read. Little bricks began to fall into place in my mind as I saw this vast machine with its skilled staff convert information into a living resource.

Not all the work I did was restricted to moving stuff around within the Palace of Westminster. One of the services which the House of Commons offers is a telephone enquiry office where straightforward accurate information is made available to the public on a day-to-day basis. This can be quite simple, like 'what is the name of my MP' and 'how do I address the envelope?' Other examples would be more complicated but the public service ethos which I knew about from the BBC meant that the few days I spent observing there made a lasting impression on me. If you hold information which rightfully belongs in the public domain, then you give it to people with minimum fuss and maximum courtesy. The Commons library is a magnificent resource, servicing both the members of Parliament and their researchers and the outside world as well. On my last day I was taken to a Commons bar overlooking the River Thames for a farewell drink and I presented my colleagues with a spoof text based on the workings of the in-house computer system. I called it, 'Not the Thought for the Day', but lurking in its subtext were the same kind of references to salvation that I usually try to broadcast about. It was a joke really but as I wrote it I could not help noticing that references to saving and help and re-cycling and so on abound on the net. It now carries scripts which once upon a time seemed to belong exclusively to the Churches. Not surprisingly the old metaphors work, even if now their meaning is assigned to the world of virtual living.

When my problems with the Vatican began, I started making contrasts in my own mind between the administration of a parliamentary democracy and the workings of the offices of the former Holy Inquisition. Idle questions floated through my mind. After all, I had never visited the Vatican, I had only stood outside. The only visit to Rome I had ever made was with my mother when I was sixteen. She took me to Italy for a month to try to cure me of my religious vocation. We visited Rome, Florence – where all the guides in the picture galleries seemed to have a thing about contact with English girls' flesh – Venice and Assisi. I had loved it and felt deeply pious as I visited churches and shrines. As a piece of propaganda, the exercise was a washout. I came back even more convinced of God's call.

No further opportunity to visit Rome had arisen. My travels took me everywhere else, but not to Italy until 1998, and then, in a sense, it was too late. So where were the files on me kept? How could I access them? And what was in them anyway? As the study of communications became more important to me so too did these questions. Vatican secrecy troubled me because it went against my own sense that no one need be afraid of information. It needs to be dealt with, obviously; and a teaching Church, such as the Roman Catholic Church, has the right to collect it. But how do you define your own orthodoxy without creating heretics? Only recently I heard a man in Cambridge walking his small son down the road. He was trying to explain the idea of heresy to him and I felt guilty for eavesdropping. 'Take Mary, for example', he said. 'If you thought she was more important than Jesus, you'd be a heretic.' 'And what would happen to me?' the little boy asked. 'You'd be burnt to death.' The little boy considered this in silence for a minute. Then his father seemed to take pity on him and said, 'But don't worry. If you were a pagan, then nothing at all would happen to you. It's only the Christians who have a bad time.' It was all I could do not to swing around in the street and smile or call out 'Exhibit A' or something.

The visit to Rome in 1998 was something of a landmark. I went with Angela Tilby, who by now had left the BBC and her work as a TV producer. She had trained for ordination in the Church of England and was duly ordained that year. We stayed at the Venerable English College and enjoyed a quality of hospitality and welcome which were like balm. Angela wanted to explore Ancient Rome as she teaches church history and needed slides to illustrate the working of the early Church. We visited catacombs together and looked at old mosaics, particularly in the Church of St Praxedes, which told a different and alternative story of the role of women in the early Church. The visual evidence at least had not been filed away. It stood there high up on the walls, well out of the way of marauding vandals and proudly proclaimed the identity of one Theodora Episcopa or Bishop Theodora.

We also went to clerical outfitters. I sat in a chair and watched, feeling slightly ambivalent, while Angela wandered up and down the racks and laden shelves. The vestments, mostly made by women let it be said, glinted at us. They were beautiful, unlike anything you could get anywhere else, with classical designs and modern dyes working together to maximum effect. Angela cannot be the first Anglican woman priest to have tried on stoles and chasubles in these bastions of priestly privilege, and, if a little twitchy, the attendants were unfailingly courteous. After all, she represented liquid cash. Yet all this was happening a stone's throw away from the monolithic centre of an organisation which recognised neither her calling nor, let it be said, her orders.

We also visited the Rome headquarters of the IBVM and again were greeted with great generosity and care. Little was said in our informal chat about my own circumstances, but after lunch I had the opportunity to state my own case and circumstances. I left feeling refreshed, though with what was now becoming a familiar feeling of dread tugging at me. In a sense the kindness had to be conditional. For I knew that in any open conflict, that is if further undue pressure came from the Vatican, I would be a casualty. It seemed to me that my spiritual task was to get my mind and heart round this. I had to accept that there was too much at stake for the other members of the community. This visit was in Easter 1998; in the summer my worst fears were realised. The formula would be simple when it came, and all the more memorable for that: 'Lavinia, we cannot support you; we have to support the Vatican.'

The previous year, when I was studying in London, all these toxic questions seemed to be a long way away. My interest in information management was real and genuine, yet it was strangely academic. I thought about orthodoxy and heresy in dispassionate terms as though I was somehow not involved. I thought about information management and the flow of ideas as though they were puzzles inside my head, and I wondered about how you would store certain categories of material, especially the bits you disagreed with. How would they fit? In my own case this was an easy question to answer because I have very few personal books. I have dictionaries of course, of history, dates, computing, quotations, popes, saints and theatre. I have the Documents of the Second Vatican Council and the Post-Conciliar Documents as they are called. I have a varied collection of prayer books to help me when I do the *Daily Service*, so hymn and service books from all our Churches. I have a small specialist collection of books about broadcasting which I collect as a hobby. But as I have always lived and worked in large institutions I have only rarely needed my own books as I have had access to excellent libraries. Everything else lives inside my head. Only suddenly it didn't, because suddenly the Internet opened up a world of information to me that lay beyond my wildest dreams.

I learnt that I had access to the remotest and most obscure concerns of learning as well as to simple and practical things like 'How do you make an Advent wreath?' This is a question I was asked by a TV production company which wanted me to start doing worship for them. Other questions came from journalist friends: give me the low-down on Pope Joan; give me information about Fatima the daughter of the Prophet. Whichever direction I looked in, information came tumbling into my lap. All my categories about orthodoxy were exploded. What I was learning is that someone who searches the Internet has a far greater sphere of moral responsibility than I had ever thought possible, and certainly greater than when the choosing of texts is done on our behalf by censors. What is called for is not so much orthodoxy as discernment. The Rule of Benedict tells us to 'listen'; here – as never before – is an opportunity to listen and to struggle to understand.

My horizons were radically changed. Suddenly I had my brand new question: how do you contain and hold information with which you disagree? With it came an instant answer that I knew I had to explore, namely the answer provided by the dynamics of the Internet. For the Internet is a living deposit of information, not a dead one. It changes shape and modifies daily. It has forced people in the academic community to realise that they are part of a worldwide community of research. With the net you can put questions online; you can share your explorations and ideas; you can e-mail colleagues with first drafts and second drafts and unlimited drafts of your work; you can invite comment and criticism; you can bring fluidity and dialogue into your creative processes. Information on the Internet dances to a different drumbeat and plays a different tune.

I think some church people are terrified of it and I long to tell them that they do not need to be, for it requires mature Christian and human behaviour of the highest calibre and is a worthy companion for our times. It is not teeming with deviants or perverts; it has the capacity to hum with angels' wings. More than that it enables us to ask the age-old questions, like 'Where is God?' and provides us with rich meta-phorical answers to them. Science has chased out our sense that God is in heaven, namely a location beyond the stars, because we know that there is no space beyond the stars for God to fit. And then along comes the Internet with its language and imagery about 'virtual reality', the realm of digits rather than atoms, and suddenly there is a mysterious realm where God may safely dwell.

In June 1998, when Cardinal Bertone's letter was copied to me, I had to take stock because – as I saw it – I stood poised on the threshold of the new informa-tion age as an honest seeker, but also as a member of a religious community and of a Church which were precious and important to me. Yet I did so as someone who stood under judgment and when the judgment came and it went against me, I had to rethink my position.

I bought time. In simple terms I refused to commit myself in public to any kind of assent, but equally I did not profess dissent. All I said openly was that I thought that it was wrong for a book which had been written in good faith to be destroyed and that I could explain quite clearly why I experienced this as a grave injustice. I reserved the pain of this experience to myself.

For I was having other ideas too. My mind could not stand still and I certainly did not want to get pinned down to my opinions on ordination or contraception when these were humming around my mind. Despite the aching depression I felt, mine were inevitably theological questions as well as purely practical ones. I should add that at this time it never entered my head to think that I might have to leave the community. I went on thinking about what most interested me, namely the proclamation of God's word in an information age. As I saw it, theology raises important questions about ideas. We ask fundamental ones, like 'What are we to believe?' and 'Why are we to believe it?' These 'what? and 'why?' questions have honest answers and fairly simple ones What we are invited to do is to proclaim the love of God. And why we proclaim this love is because the gospel tells us to. But how do we do this? And how do we do this when voices which disagree with our own emerge and when they ask different or difficult questions?

In *Woman at the Altar* I had asked different questions. Yet I had asked them in good faith. I have to concede now that when women are ordained this will come about because it is manifestly God's will, not because I or any other Catholic woman worked for it or wrote about it. So I regard myself as a speculator, as an enquirer, rather than as a political heavyweight or martyr to the cause. What I also notice is that, because I am a writer and because I use the Internet, I have access to a level of power and authority which, once upon a time, would have been refused to me. The Internet gives me access to the world. I can use it to search for information and also, as I realised when I began to design my own website, the world can also use it to access me. I wondered idly if any of the sisters I had met in China would ever use it to look at my website and to discover what had happened to me.

It seemed to me important to ask how my gifts as a communicator were to be used in the service of the Church now that I had this additional tool. I wondered if modern communications systems work to enhance the Church's legitimate authority or if they will increasingly be seen as offering an escape route to individual members who are labelled as 'dissidents' and so dismissed. The simple dichotomy I suggest here troubles me deeply because it suggests that the real victim will be the Holy Spirit and the essential Christian task of discernment. I tried typing the word 'Vatican' into a variety of Internet search engines and the results were extraordinarily diverse. The official Vatican website is buried in a massive list of sites, some of which ape and parody its concerns and contents. How is it to stand out from the crowd? How are dioceses and priests and religious orders as well as individual members of the Church to build websites which enhance the whole? Is this even possible? Or desirable?

'The Internet encourages anarchy.' 'The Internet encourages discernment.' I began to ask myself which of these two statements might be true. To the over-defensive, to totalitarian governments or organisations, the net represents anarchy because it actively encourages discussion. It enables the alternative view to be expressed and then defended. That is precisely why I believe the Internet makes the practice of discernment a necessity. It makes the searcher grow up. The teaching Church and the Internet-user do not need to war on each other. They can emerge from their respective blue and red corners and shake hands in the middle of the ring. How is this to happen?

When I teach my students in Cambridge how they can use the Internet to help them research information for essay writing, I start by getting them to list the criteria by which they can evaluate what they find. Usually they identify 'accuracy', and then they say that they need the information to be up to date. Nothing dates so quickly as old research. I type something innocuous into the search engine. Take 'teletubbies' as an example. If 15,000 hits are listed, how are they to choose which are likely to meet their criteria? The answer is simple: those sites which have the magic letters 'BBC' in their website addresses are most likely to provide authority. Equally sites which come from the academic community will have the letters 'ac' in their address if they are British and 'edu' if they are American. The language of URLs is a code to be cracked and it rapidly reveals its mysteries.

They say that you cannot judge a book by its cover, but you can discover a great deal about it by evaluating the information displayed on the cover: the name of the publishing house and the date of publication tell you about its authority and currency. So too with the world wide web. Appearance tells you something if not everything and very soon you get to know if you are dealing with some weighty organisation or a crackpot individual.

The Catholic Church has a unique role as a communicator because it is a worldwide Church. It is built upon the very notion of dispersal because the great commission given at the end of Matthew's Gospel is a command to 'go and tell all nations and baptise them in the name of the Father and of the Son and of the Holy Spirit'. My membership of this Church made me a citizen of the world. Even when I felt most alienated from its structures, I was confident that my use of the Internet made me an apostle of cyberspace. It enabled me to situate myself as someone who wanted to 'tell out my soul', or talk about the gospel in public, rather than as someone who should be silenced in the name of suspicion and fear. I have pinned my star to the world wide web by becoming *The Tablet*'s Internet reviewer; I have associated myself with the University of Edinburgh's Media and Theology Project; I have lectured widely on the topic of God and cyberspace. My investment in this world is not an attempt to cover my back against Vatican opposition. If anything I believe I am advancing the very causes which the Church claims to espouse when it preaches a doctrine of communications. The trick is to realise that this means being unafraid to embrace new truths.

10

'What is Religion for?'

What is it that the Church has to communicate,
whether on the radio, in books, in art and literature,
on TV or on the Internet, let alone in church buildings,
or by its presence on the High Street? How can this
message be renewed? The Church has a unique message, which is to say that we are made in the image and
likeness of God and that God loves us. Every time I
broadcast or write or teach, this is what I am trying to
say. At my most jaundiced, I wonder if the Christian
gospel, as many people hear it, has anything more to
offer than a diatribe about the inadequacy of women
or a commentary on sex. My anger with the Vatican,
when it appeared in my own case to reduce the whole
of Catholic truth to such trivialisation, is matched
every time I walk into a Catholic church in the UK
and find that the Catholic Truth Society pamphlets at
the back are all about abortion and contraception.
What on earth do we think we are saying to the wider
world if the whole of Christian truth is represented in
this way? What are total strangers who walk into
church looking for consolation to make of this
onslaught?

As a child I loved the Catholic Truth Society's output and never resented spending my pocket money on their pamphlets, for what I bought offered me a broad portrait and opened both my heart and my mind to the truth. Nowadays I marvel at the fidelity of the Catholic laity who struggle on through thick and thin when they are regularly offered not bread, but a stone, a burden which is put around their necks instead of a nourishing loaf to feed them.

What is the truth? What, in particular, is Catholic truth? I still agonise about these questions and do not in any way claim to have the right answer myself. Of course the Church believes that good news is about more than a tranche of ideas about women and fertility, but the 'good-news idea' or concept, so to say, namely the core teaching of the Church, surely needs to be stripped down and reassembled, reconfigured in modern dress. Christians claim to have good news to proclaim. I know about that and love it; I have been hearing that good news since before I can remember; but nowadays I want it to have real value and not to be camouflaged in pious rhetoric or sexist guff. Genuine piety has nothing to be ashamed of and neither has genuine sexuality. It is the ersatz version of Christian truth which is so draining for the life and energy of the Church.

So much so that my skin crawls when I hear the Christian gospel variously described as good news for all mankind, or good news for good people (and bad news for women or for the rest of us), or – and wait for this – good news for the poor. Draw your own conclusions at this point. Now of course I know that what I am saying here is controversial. It raises a whole sequence of questions and some of them are deeply uncomfortable. I belong to the generation of Catholics who were told that God brings good news to the poor, yet nowadays I have problems with the easy way in which these words trip off our tongues. For a start I now believe that we have to ask if God endorses the activities of special-interest groups: for minorities over majorities; for the illiterate over the literate; for the poor over the rich. Is God on the side of one lot of people over and against the rest of us?

This dualistic thinking enabled a Marxist form of social spirituality to engage the teachers of liberation theology in the 1970s and 1980s. I remember it well because it excited me and I wanted to know more about it. But nowadays I find myself with other questions. What are our moral imperatives? Are they simply about money? In which case I tremble.

Let me press my case. How can a gospel be good unless it is proclaimed to sinners? We miss the point totally if we espouse political causes and neglect the real needs of the poor, of the rich; of the outcast and the insider; of the person with HIV, the depressive, the hallucinator, the alcoholic, the spy, the thug, the unmarried mother, the drugged baby, the poor, sad, lonely git and the successful, entrepreneurial, ISA-buying, former council-house purchaser, with several K invested in a dot.com world beyond our ken. If we place poverty in one place only, namely in the idea of material poverty, we are doomed because the gospel becomes irrelevant to those who are not poor in this way. We fail to acknowledge that each of us is poor and that Jesus embraced our poverty when he assumed our humanity. To be human is to be poor as it is to be finite, rather than infinite like God. True conversion enables us to look our own poverty in the eye and to acknowledge our need for God. Only when people have experienced the utter and absolute security of conversion, of accepting that God loves them whatever they have done, will they turn around and do something for the poor.

Those of us – and I count myself in this category, because true conversion is terrifying and most of us back off from it – those of us who deny our spiritual poverty will be led blindfold as surely as Isaac, the son of Abraham, when he was consigned to slaughter at the bush of sacrifice. We will be blind victims. We will have nothing to say and nothing to offer. Our ignorance is the sin that cries out to heaven for vengeance, for it disenfranchises people. It leads us to deny the theological mystery at the heart of the incarnation. When God became man in Christ, as the Christian gospel proclaims, he stripped himself. He left heaven for earth. He abandoned the Godhead for life in Galilee. The self-stripping of God offers a radical charge to all of us, rich or poor, sick or well. Can we bear to become human? Can we bear to be ordinary? Can we bear to let go of some secret glamorous destiny that otherwise makes us, as believers, somehow assume that we are better than other people?

Now take that idea on board and you are offered a spiritual challenge that will blow your mind apart. This is about embracing the spiritual, emotional, psychological, political, social, economic, international, and so on concerns of the world on a canvas which restores the gospel to its genuine role in human discourse. This is not about trying to be relevant, or being trendy. This is about *kenosis* – and I apologise for the Greek – namely, self-emptying, displacing the centre where you think your self is located and finding it in a new place. It is about embracing faith because belief in God will do more than change your life. It will change the world. This is about accepting that sin is a genuine evil and that it is not about something which other people do; it is about what we all do all of the time. Genuinely. We are not Goody Two-Shoes, as I discovered when I was a young religious and trying desperately hard to get it right all of the time. To say that you are needy is to seek help. To say you are a sinner is to admit the grace of God. As I had discovered in my own life, the simple truth is that God loves us and forgives us all of the time, whatever our own personal pattern of order and disorder.

On a more pedestrian note, I can quite see why, during the 1960s, '70s and '80s, Christians thought that their principal task was to get involved with the concerns of the poor. I did it myself to the best of my ability. I espoused all the right causes. I bought the mug, the T-shirt (even when I was not in a position to wear it as anything except a vest under the habit), I embraced the ideology. Yet did I really embrace sinners? I am deeply troubled by this question because it cuts across all the pious rhetoric that I thought I valued at that time. In a sense I placed sin with the rich, with the successful, with the liberal and democratic political elite. Now I want to ask a much more passionate question, a core question: where does God place sin?

My question is a deeply serious one and I wrestle with it daily, especially now that I still want to 'tell out' good news yet am more keenly troubled by this question than ever. Deprived of the means that went with membership of a religious community, I am conscious that mine is a very lone voice. Deprived of the authority of having a distinctive role in the Church, I am cast back on my own resources, yet I know how frail they are. My access to the media is only guaranteed by my record as a religious broadcaster and journalist; my access to the printed word is only guaranteed by my ability to write. Both are tenuous, fragile and frail. Without either, without a microphone or a word processor, my 'apostolic' vocation, my desire to talk about the love which God has for us, would go down the tubes. I have lost my obvious platform and, in fairness, gained a new one.

For now I am able to speak freely. I am able to say what I believe and take the responsibility for this without looking over my shoulder. So the questions I find myself asking have a sharper focus as I am speaking from the heart and not from an anxious imagination, conscious that if I am not careful, the worst will happen – to me and to the community. Where does sin lie? Is a good life about trying to be squeaky clean, or about honesty and truth? And what about my serious questions: what news is good nowadays and how can it best be proclaimed? As I have often asked myself, 'What is religion for?'

An ironical aside. As a child, when I was at the convent in Edgbaston, my class performed a play. I had a semi-star role, so my name was mentioned in the programme. So too was the name of the star from the Senior School: Karen Armstrong, well known nowadays as a former nun who has gone on to apply her formidable mind to understand the workings of faith, of God and of fundamentalism. My mother kept records of all the family's performances as school children so I have the copy that says that Karen Armstrong was St Francis in the Senior School play and I was the sister of Moses in what the Junior School offered on the same occasion. As I say, this aside adds an ironical twist to my tale because Karen Armstrong has pursued questions like these in print more intelligently and honestly that I could ever aspire to do, and she too is a former member of a religious community. She is living proof that the academic life goes on, whatever our life choices.

In February 1997 I asked the question publicly: 'What is religion for?' The occasion was the University Mission in Cambridge. Great St Mary's, the University Church where I had preached at Ruth Morgan's memorial service, was once again packed. The deans and chaplains who choose a theme for a Mission such as this had chosen 'Unmasking Faith'. The idea of unmasking captured my imagination. How about unmasking religion? For a University Mission is a call to faith, a deliberate attempt to put the words from Matthew's Gospel about going out and preaching the good news into practice. I launched in.

The very first words God speaks in the Bible are words of permission. God says 'Let there be,' and issues a call, an invitation, into being. So along come the light, the plants and the animals. And then on a Friday afternoon – for we really are a Friday afternoon job – along come human beings: called into being, called into existence, made in the divine image and likeness. God is revealed to us and we are revealed to God.

Then what are the second words that God speaks in the Bible? Well, most memorably, the Word becomes flesh. God is revealed as the God of desire who sends his only Son into the world as our Saviour. God sends the divine Son, made in the divine image and likeness, to take us to the place of salvation, where our true image is restored to us and we can let go of the masks that we usually use.

The point that I was making is that the Word is made flesh. The doctrine of the incarnation means that God is spoken into our midst. A theology of Christian presence in the world, let alone communications, which takes this doctrine seriously has to grapple with ideas about why we are here, whether we appear on a concert programme as Armstrong or Byrne, or as great players in the world of commerce and international development. Is it surprising, given the date, that I went on to say to my listeners and to myself:

I have been asking myself a very serious question over the last year: 'What is religion for?' And if I come before you this evening as someone who is trying to unmask faith, then I have to say that I now realise that

I have been giving three answers to it in my own life. When I was a young nun, I thought religion was to make you good. And actually I was not unmasked, because I was so terrified of my own badness, that I thought it essential to have a mask on so that it would look as though I was trying really hard to please God, to please other people, to serve other people, to have a kind of shiny-white template that looked OK and where nobody could catch me out. But I could not in fact take the risk of unmasking. I couldn't unmask to myself. I couldn't unmask to other people for the simple reason that I was convinced that religion was to make you good, was meant to make you good.

Think what that does to your vision of God. In fact you are afraid of God, because God knows the truth about you. So you can never go completely freely to prayer because you feel you are going to be judged. God can get behind the mask. What does it do to your understanding of the Bible? I think the Bible becomes a sort of magic book where you go and look for proof texts that prove your thesis, that God is good and that you have to be good. It is all about good. You persecute yourself in the name of a total unreality. I see a huge amount of this in national life at the moment. It seems to me an absolute delusion to say that we can have transparency, as though each of us is like a stick of rock, with 'goodness, goodness, goodness', written all the way through, with no murky bits and bits that have gone a bit squiffy.

But at the time I was quite sustained by that vision: that religion is something designed to make us good. So though I look back at that time with a certain amount

of horror – Goody Two-Shoes, being very unreal, trying
desperately hard – I also try to look upon that person
with a certain amount of affection. I give her ten on ten
for effort, zero on ten for other things, like honesty.

Then I suppose the next thing I began to think about
when I thought about religion and its task in our lives
– to unmask faith – was that religion allows you to say
you're bad. Quite uniquely religion allows you to say 'I
am a sinner, and I am loved and forgiven by God, and
I am quirky, and I am dishonest, and I get moody, and
sometimes I don't want to get up in the morning, and
I'm economical with the truth.' i.e. I am a real person.
Those words of God at the beginning of the Bible, the
call into being, 'Let there be' are not a call into 'Let
there only be good people and good things'. They are
about a call to admit the extraneous, the problematical:
'Let there be creepy crawlies' as well. And let me have
the honesty to say that they are in me too. The Irish poet
Yeats put it in a wonderful line of verse:

> I must lie down where all the ladders start
> In the foul rag and bone shop of the heart.

Until you know you have a foul rag and bone shop of a
heart, no ladder, no Jacob's ladder, can be planted in
your life. It was only when Jacob was absolutely vile,
foul to his brother, when he went to a place that was
distressing to him, when he faced the crossing of the
river, transition, shame, that he could lie down, put his
head on a stone, on a hard place, and that a ladder
could be built in his heart and angels could go up and
down and move between him and God.

If you had asked me at that time what I thought God was like, I would have been much freer to tell you something about my experience of God as loving, truly loving, truly knowing, a God of forgiveness, a God who I didn't have to mask up in front of, because I was known, who I didn't have to be afraid of, because I was known, judged, forgiven, loved. The old hymn put it in those words 'ransomed, healed, restored, forgiven'. And that's the package: Jesus Christ meets your desire to live for ever. At that time a real relationship with Jesus becomes possible. He is our friend, he is our brother, he is our lover. He went to the cross so that we should have that experience of God as the one who judges, heals, restores, redeems us. We are safe with God, with Jesus.

We are safe with the Bible, for goodness' sake, because we can begin to read it in a much deeper, more interesting and ambivalent way. We can find some of the horrors in it: I've mentioned Jacob. I could talk about David. I could talk about Elijah – not when he is doing that magnificent act with the fire: we all know about that. We can all do prophets of Baal stuff, where you go 'Zap' and get the fire up and running. But what happens next? He goes out into the desert and he keeps lying down and saying 'Ah, my God, I'm depressed. I could die.' And he says something extraordinary: 'I am no better than my ancestors.' He accepts his humanity. Up to that moment we didn't know Elijah had ancestors. He was just the man who appeared from nowhere, no family, no background, no smirch in the background, no dysfunction behind him, but this sort of super-wise fellow. But then he goes out into the wildernesss. He lies down. God has to keep appointing, 'ordaining' it used to say in the old days in some of the Bibles, 'the Lord appointed' or 'the Lord ordained a mustard seed'. (Some of our difficulties about what we have been ordaining recently pale into insignificance when you think God can ordain mustard seeds!) God appoints – ordains the mustard seed that takes care of Elijah, but then it withers and he gets to shout at God.

Now once you allow yourself exposure to the real people in the Bible you then begin to discern that God too is not quite the happy bunny he was cracked up to be. God, too, is very ambivalent about human beings. There was a terrible movement about ten years ago to produce sanitised versions of the Psalms, where all the ugly, angry bits got cut out, and God was all sweetness and light. It is terribly difficult to come to God genuinely in prayer if you have to be benign. Whereas if you can come and rattle the bars and say 'This hurts, and I'm angry about that, and I'm in a mess', then something authentic begins to happen and there's ladders get put in between us, the foul rag and bone shop of the heart, and God. Jesus Christ meets our desire to live for ever.

I could leave you there and we could do some more reflection about that. But over the last six months, my idea of what religion is for, my own personal unmasking of faith, has actually moved on a bit further. And I think I need to tell you about it, because I'd be selling you short if I merely said, 'What's wonderful about Christianity is that it lets me say I'm bad as well as I'm good.' For there is a further unmasking. If you ask me now what religion is for, I think that religion uniquely brings us into the presence of the transcendent God.

*That is the unmasking of faith. We stand on holy
ground. And we need to know that we do that. That is
the message that our world needs to hear. We stand on
holy ground, the place of encounter between us and God.*

I retract none of that now. If you stand on holy ground
in the presence of God, then you have another theological insight which cuts to the heart of Christian
living, let alone to the heart of the Christian communications debate. For you are blinded by the light of
what you see and it makes everything else seem
relative. If religion exists to bring us into the presence
of God, then we can let go of our need to terrorise
those who do not think like us and embrace them as
fellow searchers, trying to respect the integrity of their
consciences and their journey to God. As a Christian
communicator as well as a believer, I am concerned to
think about ways in which this experience can be
communicated on the radio or TV or the Internet and
so on.

So far, religious broadcasting has taken its style and
flavour from the work of the BBC. But there are new
developments and many of these have been led by
evangelicals who are keen to get God on air or on the
box at whatever cost. The results can be mind-numb-
ing as more and more well-suited men come out and
tell you what to believe and how to live your life.
Sadly, too, some of the Christian discussion which
happens on mainstream TV makes good watching
only because it is adversarial and nothing is so much
fun as watching people getting red with anger as they
put down their enemies under their feet with argu-

ments drawn from the Scriptures. I am always irritated when I hear church leaders attacking the Internet as a smutty collection of sites full of pornography and raging paedophiles. The truth is far more subtle than that. Over a quarter of its sites are about health issues, for example, not just sex. Moreover, religion too is big on the net as there are over 20 million Christian sites, 7 million Muslim and 4 million Jewish ones. Religion is just as significant and controversial on the world wide web as sex is.

So what kind of theology might drive a new vision of Christian communications? The mandate comes from the words of Jesus: we are to 'go and teach all nations'. I share that call with all Christians, but in my case it is nuanced because the initial religious impulse or vocation comes from a different place. I do not see myself standing on some Galilean hillside, part of a mass of followers, all of whom are wearing spiked boots and preparing to dash off to 'do good'. If I can say this without sounding too precious, my own sense of call has a different starting point. In his *Spiritual Exercises*, Ignatius of Loyola has the exercitant or person making the retreat eavesdrop on an extra-ordinary conversation. He wants the retreatant to think about the incarnation, about the moment when the word became flesh. For most of us that would mean contemplating the account of the angel Gabriel's visit to Mary, given in Luke's Gospel; for some of us it might mean a visit to a mental art gallery, to a place in our imaginations where we can recall one of the old masters which depict this scene. So we might stand in awe gazing at Fra Angelico's work from Florence or recall a personal favourite – and my own would be the alabaster representation of an alarmed-looking Mary from the side of a tomb in Wells Cathedral. Either way, we would turn to art for inspiration.

Ignatius does something quite different and this is one of the reasons why I am so drawn to his spiritual path. For he suggests that in our imaginations we should go back to the beginning, to the moment when, within the Godhead, the three Divine Persons look out from heaven to consider a world in need. This is what he says in his 'Contemplation on the Incarnation':

> *FIRST POINT. This will be to see the different persons: First, those on the face of the earth, in such great diversity in dress and in manner of acting. Some are white, some black; some at peace, and some at war; some weeping, some laughing; some well, some sick; some coming into the world, some dying; etc.*
>
> *Secondly, I will see and consider the Three Divine Persons seated on the royal dais or throne of the Divine Majesty. They look down upon the whole surface of the earth, and behold all nations in great blindness, going down to death and descending into hell.*
>
> *Thirdly, I will see our Lady and the angel saluting her.*
>
> *I will reflect upon this to draw profit from what I see.*

The language is quaint but the insight is dramatic. For here we share in the vision of God and we look down with God from heaven; our desire to communicate in God's name is driven by human need, not by any romantic illusions we might have dreamed up on our own. Not only are we to look, but, as Ignatius tells us, we are to listen. It is not enough to watch, as though this were a silent movie. For the Divine Persons within the Blessed Trinity are talking to each other. They decide that the Second Person should be sent down to earth for our redemption. Only then does Ignatius, with all the skill of a TV producer or film-maker, 'cut' to the small room in Nazareth where Mary awaits the angel's visit. According to this reading, Ignatius sees the incarnation as part of a much greater and wider dynamic. It is the work of the Trinity made flesh. How do we know this? Because we have heard the Divine Persons talking to each other. Communication originates in heaven and not on earth. To communicate is to share in the very life of God.

No wonder the earliest Jesuits, such as Francis Xavier, went to the ends of the known world. Of course theirs was missionary work but the dynamic which drove it was about being part of the conversation of God. As well as proclaiming the cross and resurrection of Jesus – the obvious focus of mission – they would inevitably preach and live out the incarnation. At times they would take risks. They would go native – like Matteo Ricci who dressed for all the world as a Chinese mandarin; they would engage with the struggle for justice of local peoples, as in Paraguyan settlements or reductiones; they would risk martyrdom, as in El Salvador. The journey would be their home.

11

A Year in Limbo

I must be a slow learner for it took me a full year to internalise the actual impact of what had been happening to me and to my sense of God's call within the fabric and everyday events of my own life. Because of the effect of Cardinal Hume's intervention I had no further reprimands from Rome, no more demands that I should sign up to this or to that, no more confrontations. I was off the hook. But the Vatican's silence too was a burden in its own right. No one wrote to me to say that my troubles were over; no one said that the demand for a public declaration of assent had been dropped; no one said sorry that your books were pulped or burnt or whatever. I found myself feeling more and more disenfranchised, as though the Church and I were operating on different wavelengths, and an unspoken pact had been brokered which I did not really understand. Their silence somehow committed me to keep silent in turn.

I continued to do my job, I taught my students, wrote *The Dome of Heaven*, signed a contract to produce another prayer book similar to it, only this time for everyday use, and kept my head down. The depression began to lift and in its place I felt a kind of numb perseverance. Then came an invitation out of the blue. I was to go to Peru and to speak at a conference there, which was organised by a non-governmental organisation called Tramas. It was about gender, power and love. I left on a dull November day in 1999, flying, as I thought, to the sun.

Lima is a sprawling cloud-covered city, a city of huge contrasts in a vast remote land. I was collected at 4 a.m. at the airport by a priest whom I had met in the UK where he worked in the East End of London. He was grateful for the bottle of whisky I brought him and dropped me off at the IBVM community house where I was to stay. The sisters had got up specially to greet me and led me to my room. There were two Europeans and two Peruvians, one from the mountains and one from the jungle, as she proudly described it. The cockerels who scrabbled in the dust at the back of the house were just beginning their dawn chorus. I climbed into bed and slept like a log.

Two days later I spoke to a group of sisters who work in Lima, and who had gathered anonymously so that I could give them a paper which I was to deliver at the Tramas conference. The Catholic Archbishop of Lima is a member of the right-wing group Opus Dei and these sisters were clearly accustomed to keeping a low profile. They came from Australia, Spain, Ireland and America as well as from Peru. I felt huge admiration for them and marvelled when they told me what they did. Their work put them on the fringes, and I was greatly helped to be able to share ideas with them. I had to give two papers at the conference and had only written the first as I wanted to develop my ideas while in Peru and not simply to dish up something prepared in England. The experience of writing 'Thought for the Day' scripts for instant consumption leaves you with the desire to hold off until the last moment, in case there is something instantaneous to say. So what they had to say in the discussion we had after I had spoken fired me up. It gave me fresh impetus and fed new ideas into my second paper.

After visiting these sisters I was taken into the poorest sections of the city to see ramshackle projects where, for instance, babies were cared for so that their mothers could work; or twelve-year-olds could learn computer skills on old Apple Macs donated by some bank. The sisters were the driving force behind this work and were determined to get it right. Of course they were politicised; theirs was a campaign for justice, not a vicarage tea party. Theirs was a new way of being women religious, light years away from community recreation and the clatter of knitting needles over the crossword puzzle. I liked what I saw. As I tasted the vile jelly drink I was given when I visited the babies or drank down the yellow-coloured 'Inca Cola' which is Peru's substitute for the 'real thing', I felt the life-blood flow back into my own sense of vocation and call. Here was an active form of church community which was not afraid to take its gloves off and roll up its sleeves and do things which would make a difference to the way people lived. It was quite evident to me that these women were doing the work of priests as they went about doing good, initiating change, reconciling people with God. The only dimension of their priestly ministry which was missing, or rather withheld from them, was the ability to celebrate the sacraments with their people.

Then came another very distinctive experience, another piece of the journey which I had never anticipated and which would give me a major jolt. For I went up to the old Inca city of Cusco in the mountains, got severe altitude sickness and had a bad scare about death. After that my sense of what I could or should say in public was, as it were, taken out of my own hands. I could not look back. The Tramas conference organisers had fixed for me to set off with two fellow delegates, namely a Frenchman and an American, to visit Machu Pichu, the great Inca shrine. We were to spend three days up in Cusco, which lies 3,310 metres above sea level. We flew out of Lima on an early morning flight and were taken to a lovely hotel. So far no problems. I registered nothing. I did not take in the fact that the flight had to be so early in the morning because no planes land in Cusco after 12 noon as the atmosphere at this high altitude cannot support them. I did not know why I felt light headed and imagined this was because I had drunk the cola tea which was pressed on me when I arrived. 'Drink a lot of cola tea and you will feel fine,' the sisters had told me back down in Lima and this I duly did, as it was offered free in the hotel foyer.

Then our guide joined us and we set off in a car to go sightseeing. I gasped at the spectacular views; I marvelled at the beautiful colours of the native women's dresses and their children's clothes; I stroked a llama and bought fabulous chilli spices in the market place. Then my head and stomach fell apart and, as we returned to the hotel, I began to feel ominously ill. A young man was trying to sell me postcards as we got out of our car and headed back into the building. I stood with one hand against the wall and started to throw up. 'Look at this view,' he insisted, as the jelly and Inca Cola began their lurid return journey to earth. Just before I fainted, our guide got me inside and called for oxygen. I breathed deeply from the mask and wanted to die.

Up in my bedroom things did not improve. Then the doctor arrived and began a fantastic routine of care for me. I cannot remember his name but he asked me mine and when I said 'Lavinia' insisted on calling me 'Lady' or 'Lady Lavinia' for the rest of the evening. He called on me three times over the next four hours. First he wrote out a prescription for over two hundred dollars' worth of medicine and dispatched a porter to buy it. Then he set up my room as a hospital ward. I had altitude sickness and needed rapid intervention. He put a needle into the back of my hand to get me on to a drip and then began monitoring my heart and oxygen intake. The drip was a bit of a menace at first as he could not get the bag of fluid to hold up on the metal bracket which the hotel had provided. So he asked me if I could lend him a shoelace and used that to fix the problem. I laughed momentarily and told him that I taught communications. I have always insisted to my students that there is a hi-tech and also a lo-tech answer to every communications problem and that the gifted communicator will unerringly know which to choose. Here was my teaching being enacted before my very eyes.

Then, as I lay alone in the semi-dark, over 6,300 miles from home, away from any known contacts, I fixed my eyes on the shoelace which I had bought in the market in Cambridge, breathed deeply from the oxygen mask and wondered about life and death. This was a turning point and when I slept I did so uneasily, feeling very vulnerable and exposed.

In the morning the doctor visited again and I was allowed up. The ordeal was over but it had made an important impact on me. I have never been so far from home and so near to calamity. I felt desperately tired and older and wearier and wiser when I made my way down to Machu Pichu in the train with the others the following day and gazed on the Inca ruins and contemplated their meaning. As the American who was with me said, 'this is a place where you could pray', but who would you pray to, I wondered, and what would you pray for? When I lay under the oxygen mask I found myself saying very simple prayers, the familiar prayers from childhood. I did not pray to be spared; I simply prayed so as to talk to God. At Machu Pichu, I felt that I was in the grip of something primordial, for the people who settled there built themselves an impermeable stronghold that was clearly intended to last for ever. They must have had a sustaining vision, a cult and a culture that gave their lives meaning. Yet they left no record of it because they had no alphabet and did not write. The sheer ravishing beauty of the landscape could not, in itself, satisfy the deepest longings of their souls. Yet all trace of this has vanished and we are left with ambivalent signs about their understanding of birth and life and death. The artefacts have all gone.

I touched the delicate green lichen on the wall beside our path for reassurance. Lichen, as a plant form, is millions of years old and part of a greater destiny than I could dream about. I found God more accessible in the particular, in the lichen, than in the generalised phenomenon of the beauty of the place. I looked down at my shoes and checked the laces. Yes, they were there and I was back on track. In the photos my colleagues took that day, I look quite healthy, all signs of my altitude sickness cast aside; in reality though I had had a rendezvous with death and wanted to have no more to do with it or with its trappings. I went back down to the conference in Lima with hope and expectation. It took place in a smart hotel in Miraflores, on a street where the houses of the rich are defended by armed gunmen and the very poor are kept at bay.

The President of Peru appeared for the opening ceremony on the first day. I watched him live and then saw the whole thing over again on the TV in my hotel bedroom that evening. Politicians from all over Latin American and beyond were there; delegates included a woman General from the American Army, native women from the mountains to the north of the country in their highly embroidered clothes, medics, lawyers, academics, people from the world of commerce and the arts – and not a single priest or bishop in sight. I felt maddened and frustrated by this. The Vatican will send delegates to United Nations conferences, such as the Conference on Women that was held in Beijing in 1996. They use their influence to uphold traditional Catholic teaching on birth control, and are better known for that than for their intervention on the causes of world poverty. But at least they are there, so they get to hear what is being said by people who hold opposing views. In Lima, the conference was principally organised by a Jewish woman, Sonia Goldenberg. She had accompanied President Fujimori to Beijing and was a great mover and shaker. By attending the opening of the conference the President was endorsing her and her work. The Church clearly wanted to have nothing to do with it.

Yet the material was of critical importance to those whose interest and concern is with human morality and the way in which women and men can work together. There were sessions on gender, on men, on women, on relationships in the workplace and the home. There were sessions on power and its equitable distribution. Eminent sociologists spoke passionately about love and how it should be interpreted on the brink of the new millennium.

When I came to speak, I found that the checks I had placed on myself were no longer tenable. I had to say what I thought; I could no longer keep silence. Not only was I 6,000 miles from home, I was 6,000 miles from Rome. It was as though I felt that the long arm of the Vatican could not stretch this far. So I stood up and for the first time since I had consented to the prohibition on speaking about women and ordination in public, I said what was on my heart.

What will power look like in the twenty-first century?

This is a critical question and one which I am delighted to address. But what about the Church? As a Roman Catholic woman, I inhabit one of the few remaining social or political institutions which systematically excludes women from its structures. The Church claims absolute moral authority, yet its decisions are made by men, behind closed doors; the money is banked by men, in secret vaults; the theology which stakes out our place in public or private life is constructed by men, independently of us. There is no true sense of collaboration and partnership. The ethic is based on a 'solid state' version of human and social truth, so teaching about contraception, abortion, homosexuality, divorce, re-marriage is cast in stone.

Women are silenced in church, as in synagogue, mosque and temple. There is no place for our contribution. Yet I am encouraged by the words of the English Cardinal, John Henry Newman: 'To be human is to change; to be perfect is to have changed often'. So I would ask a simple question. Is it not dangerous for the whole of society that the Catholic Church is irredeemably sexist?

Think about how power is used in your own context. Think of the constraints that attempt both to exalt you and to silence you. Some may be religious, some political, some social. I think the religious ones are by far the hardest to deal with, because there is such emotional pressure for believers to conform to them. I want to quote to you from something which John Paul I, that Pope with a smiling face, wrote when he was still a Cardinal:

The husband ... will always want his spouse to have a beautiful appearance and a beautiful figure, to move graciously and to dress elegantly; he will also be proud if she has read Shakespeare and Tolstoy, but he is also practical and likes to eat well so he will be doubly happy if he discovers that in addition to a beautiful spouse he has acquired a priceless queen of the kitchen and queen of the sparkling floors and of a house made beautiful by delicate hands and of children brought up as living flowers.

No wonder I am scandalised when a friend says to me, 'when I go to church, I feel I have to leave my brain outside'. What a waste of talent. And also what a waste of something we should truly treasure. Because I also want to say to you that I believe the voices of women to be distinctive. We are more than cooks and cleaners and child-raisers. We do have something different to say.

So what would that be? What is the distinctive contribution of women to the dialogue of human life and discourse? What is it that is unique in what we have to say? Endless research demonstrates that women are good at multi-tasking. We know how to have several projects on the go at the same time because our brains can operate in both hemispheres at once. In today's hectic and complicated world, this is a skill to be treasured. We are good at communications. We know how to listen and how to use words as a relational tool. We are committed to relationships and bond and network instinctively. Again these are skills which can only enhance the life of the whole human family. These gifts are needed in the public domain as well as in the private one which, traditionally, has been our sphere of excellence.

So what happens when these skills are released into church life, or into any organisation which has favoured the contribution of men over women? The Church of England has now been ordaining women to the priesthood since 1994. Other Churches, the so-called 'Free' or disestablished Churches, have been ordaining in the UK since 1917. We now have documentary evidence which can help us assess the contribution of women once they are given a voice within the male establishment. You will notice that I am working from the assumption that it is only women who are ordained who can contribute fully to church life. Now you may disagree with that point, but I maintain that women – and that means the nuns and devout lay people – will always be seen in an ancillary role, until our equal status as representatives of Christ is formally recognised. This is true universally.

When the first women were ordained, as when women first became members of Parliament or lawyers or doctors, they seemed simply to replicate the system. They dressed and spoke and acted like the men and were keen to be included in the male discourse. There were those who argued that they had, as it were, simply joined the boys' club. I think that they felt judged by this verdict. Those of us who are on the outside have no idea how difficult it is for women to be heard when they enter a totally male establishment. So pain and distress accompany the sense of grace and of blessing.

Now that a critical mass of women have been

ordained, now that we have reached the tipping point, there is a change of mood. The role of priest is being feminised. It is becoming increasingly clear that the taboos which kept women away from the altar are of human rather than divine origin. So this is a story about all of us, not just about a few of us – that is to say, those women in the episcopal Churches who have vocations to the priesthood. This is a story about all women who seek to speak authoritatively from within their own experience, women who aspire to share their power rather than to exercise it over and above and against the power of men.

Is this why the Anglican woman theologian and detective-story writer, Dorothy L. Sayers, could write,

Perhaps it is no wonder that the women were first at the cradle and last at the cross. They had never known a man like this man – there never has been such another. A prophet and teacher who never nagged them, never flattered or coaxed or patronised, who never made arch jokes about them, never treated them either as, 'The women, God help us', or 'The ladies, God bless them!'; who rebuked without querulousness and praised without condescension; who took their questions and arguments seriously; who never mapped out their sphere for them, never urged them to be feminine or jeered at them for being female; who had no axe to grind and no uneasy male dignity to defend; who took them as he found them and was completely unselfconscious. There is no act, no sermon, no parable, in the whole Gospel that borrows its pungency from female perversity; nobody

*could possibly guess from the words and deeds of
Jesus that there was anything 'funny' about women's
nature.*

Dorothy L. Sayers, Are Women Human?
(*Eerdmans, 1971*)

*Dorothy L. Sayers was born in 1893. Her father was
an Anglican priest. She read modern languages at
Oxford and translated Dante. Here was a woman who
discovered the sound of her own voice and revelled in it.
I have said that we are a hostage to fortune when
religious, social and political voices crowd out our own.
There are other constraints too, economic ones for
instance. What does help us though? What are the
distinctive contributions which the twentieth century
has made to the life of women? Well, obviously, the
mechanisation of domestic work has transformed us all.
In the western world, women now have more time and
energy to devote to other tasks. In the developing world,
the pattern is more complex. So-called progress is a
mixed blessing when it brings poverty and AIDS in its
wake. But at least we are all aware. I would argue that
of the two great scientific revolutionary changes which
have transformed our life this century, the first, the
moon landing, is probably the most important. It has
changed our world view. It has made us all equal; we
are all inhabitants of this frail bluey-green marble
hanging in the sky. What happens to women in Peru
matters to me as I sit at my computer in Cambridge. I
can even see pictures of you over the Internet because of
the global technology revolution that has followed in the
wake of the moon landings. What of the other great*

scientific changes? Well, the other one which has most affected the life of women is the invention of the contraceptive pill. Whether you are for it or against it, whether you are successfully involved in natural family planning or not, this is a landmark invention and one which marks out a new moral universe for women. We have control over our own fertility and are fired up as never before.

For too long men have had control over women's bodies, women's fertility, women's ideas, women's minds. I am becoming impatient and I know that I am not alone when I protest at the sheer injustice of this. As we approach the third millennium I want to do so in the name of an empowerment of women which is not afraid to call God to be our witness. We need equality; we want recognition; we deserve acclaim. Our voices want to sing the new song of a new century. So I want to say, 'listen to us and learn from us in all our diversity'.

The taboo was broken. I had spoken in public and I had talked both about the ordination of women and about birth control. Because I was so far away from home, because the audience was sympathetic, I could speak freely at last. So what happened? Did the sky fall in? Did the floor swallow me up? I looked again at my laces; they were still attached to my shoes. I breathed deeply and thought, I could actually get some energy back and enjoy myself. I seized the moment along with the microphone and spoke from the heart. When the Congregation for the Doctrine of the Faith asked me to make a public declaration of assent to the Catholic Church's official teaching on reserving priestly ordination to men only and on artificial birth control, I knew that I was being put on the line. I had no idea that I would break rank and do so in such a public setting as a major international conference in Peru. Here was the public declaration they had asked for; it did not appear in quite the form which they had anticipated or required of me.

In Lima, in fact, I found myself pushing the argument. If the Church wants to be taken seriously by the faithful and especially by women, then it has to listen to the voices and experience of women who are not practising its teaching as well as those who are. The journey to Peru established itself as something of a landmark in my psyche. In its own way, that alien hotel bedroom or sickroom in Cusco became a kind of home to me. It sheltered and protected me when I walked in the valley of the shadow of death and gave me the courage to go out and say what I really believed. To say that is not to claim that I thought I was right and that everyone else was wrong. I had opened a gateway in my heart and imagination and recommitted myself to a conversation which I believed to be critical. Where would that lead me?

As I flew back to the UK I felt quite serene. I had had a liminal experience in Peru because I had been dangerously ill and I had survived; I had mixed with interesting people – women and men – who shared my passions and believed them to be of critical importance for the life of the nation; I had found the courage to speak candidly about what I believed. I had proclaimed the gospel and spoken about the life of faith in a secular gathering where all other church voices were absent or silent. Now I had a problem. How on earth could I reconnect to the other identity which I had in the UK, an identity which felt like a worn-out overcoat, because it was based on denial and a silence which had become too costly to keep?

12

The Journey is My Home

The final crunch came at Christmas time, as the new millennium was set to break. I was in America, not working this time, but on vacation and so in recovery mode. I stayed with one of my oldest friends, a devout Catholic, and her husband and family. We exchanged gifts. I took them wine and a proper Christmas pudding. They gave me a padded jacket – which I have worn daily ever since – and oodles of hospitality. It should have been perfect, only I was miserable. At last I was on holiday; at last I had time to think. Their home was thirty miles from crowded bustling Manhattan, yet set in parkland and overlooking a lake. It was, for all the world, like a garden unenclosed. I walked by the lakeside with Perdita and Romeo, their dogs, and wondered what on earth I should do. I took a photograph which I have since had enlarged and framed. It shows the amazingly tranquil surface of the lake, dead-leaved trees fringing its mid-blue water, the vegetation on the opposite shore reflected in the waters, the sun catching a golden-branched bush in the foreground and promising the life and renewal of a fresh spring. This is a snapshot of my condition at that moment. Did it represent a sudden hush, more winter, or what? Browns and golds and blues playing together uncertainly with not so much as a blush of green. Yet stillness and increasing certainty and, as I now see it when I look at the photo in my Cambridge study, the promise of a wide-open future, of a new start.

I swam indoors in the pool, blanking out the silence with loud music from a radio station that played 'Jingle-bell Rock' over and over again on the hi-fi speakers. I tried to forget the pain I felt. I sat and played with my laptop computer, not writing anything, just tinkering away and installing yet more and more recovery software, programmes with names like First Aid or Oil Change. I was oblivious of the fact that it was the inside of my head which needed re-formatting because its messages were tormenting me: 'Lavinia, we cannot support you; we have to support the Vatican.' Here I was in a normal household with normal people who had ordinary healthy reactions to things. At first I felt completely defeated and simply wanted to cringe because my own spirit was so bruised. Then gradually, like the hidden roots in the undergrowth in my photograph, I came back to life again. I accepted that the IBVM community had no choice but to abandon me and to support the Congregation for the Doctrine of the Faith, so great was its influence and its power to destroy. That is where the real tragedy lies.

Help came from an unexpected source. I had taken my Advent book, *The Dome of Heaven*, to the States with me so that I could continue with its readings and exercises while I was there. I had written the book to help people prepare for the new millennium by reflecting prayerfully on their own circumstances. Gradually, as I prayed with it myself, the penny began to drop in my subconscious as the events of my own life swam into the orbit of these prayers. After all, what had I written and why? Surely there was advice here which I myself needed to hear:

The day has dawned; the Morning Star has risen in our hearts and it has three meanings for us. It is first and foremost a person, Jesus our Messiah and Saviour, who was born, died and rose for us and now shines in the dome of heaven. Then it is a gospel, a proclamation, a banner headline which says that God loves us unconditionally and that we can turn to God in absolute confidence and hope. Finally, it is a vision, something which continues to draw us, just as the Magi were driven on in pursuit of the infinitely desirable, yet utterly unknown. We can journey forwards in the inner world, into undiscovered dreams and hopes, into a relationship with God which is beyond our control, yet which depends on a simple 'yes' from us, a commitment to let go and let God move in mysterious ways to transform us.

We can also journey forwards in the outer world, taking care to 'grow and become strong, filled with wisdom' (Luke 2:40), just as the boy Jesus did, so that 'the favour of God' might be upon us. This means taking risks, as the Magi did. It means letting go of some of our deepest and more tenderly held convictions. It means exposing our minds to new ideas, even ones which stretch and trouble us. It means being deeply committed to reconciliation, so that we will journey out in the name of this goal, even if our journey takes us a long way from home. It means new encounters and finding that things are, in T. S. Eliot's word, 'satisfactory'. It means the ultimate encounter with Jesus who comes as our judge and merciful friend, the one who waits for us, Jesus whose Spirit first placed the gift of faith in our hearts and called us to roam under the dome of heaven, searching for a person, an experience and now a new vision to strengthen us for a new millennium.

When I first wrote those words I had no idea that I might possibly be writing them to myself; that it was I who would have to journey forwards both in the inner and the outer worlds. After all, I was landlocked into a conflict which was not of my own making, but one which I thought I could weather by keeping silent about it. Yet as the New Year dawned, as I looked into the future, standing, as I did now, at the turn of a new century and a new millennium, I realised that I could not go on. I talked freely with Amanda and David, my hosts, and found myself saying that I would have to leave the community. They looked mightily relieved because they were more aware of what was going on than I was, for they knew that I was miserable and angry and a burden to myself as well as to other people.

On my return to England, when I began to negotiate my withdrawal from the IBVM, I read that extract from *The Dome of Heaven*, with tears pouring down my face, to the group of sisters who were responsible for my departure, in the sense that it had to be brokered with them. They listened in silence. This was all I had to offer by way of explanation for what I was doing, but I offered it in good faith and from what was now an unburdened heart. I was asking to leave the community because I could no longer bear to be part of an institution which had, of necessity, to uphold bits of Catholic teaching which were being used to persecute me and my conscience and the consciences of thousands of women who thought like me. Better to be out and sane than to remain in and go mad with the compromise of silence that was forced upon me.

So what triggered the final decision? What pushed me over the edge? Firstly, I think the genuine sense of misery that the 'burning' of the book and the bullying attitude of the Congregation for the Doctrine of the Faith had engendered in me. I had become too unhappy to go on as I was. Secondly, the sense that silence was killing me, that I had to be able to speak freely about the position of women in the Church without dragging the good name of the community down with me. And thirdly, the conviction that there genuinely was a new beginning here, that a new millennium offered a fresh start.

Then came a newspaper report that set off a chain reaction in my head. I read in *The New York Times* that there had been 3 million Roman Catholics in church on Christmas Day in New York City alone. I was staggered by this statistic and stopped to think about what this could mean in financial terms. If each of them gave a dollar bill to the collection plate, that would mean $3 million, just like that. It being

Christmas, though, some of them might be more generous. Let's say that the collection in New York City alone netted $10 million. That is serious money. Now visualise these good devout Catholic parishioners coming into church for their Christmas celebrations. They would arrive in families, huddled groups seeking shelter from the cold outside and then arranging themselves in the pews: mom, pop and a couple of children – living testimony to the practice of what? Birth control.

Families like that of my grandfather's mother with her seventeen offspring no longer exist in the Catholic world. Whether we like it or not most Catholic families do practise birth control; many or even most of them practise artificial birth control. The evidence is there for all to see. Yet they arrive in church, seek forgiveness, give generously, receive communion and go home and begin all over again. Do they get penalised? Are they asked to make public declarations of assent to this or that? The answer is no. Ten million dollars is a great deal of money. And that is only on Christmas Day. Multiply that by the other fifty-one weeks of the year and you get staggering amounts of money.

Yet write a book in which you argue that along with space travel, the invention of the contraceptive pill was a transforming moment of the twentieth century and you get quite different treatment, as I had discovered to my cost. Write a book in which you lay out the arguments for the ordination of women and you meet a brick wall. The wheels were spinning in my head now and I saw that there was no way forward but out. I had ended *The Dome of Heaven* with prophetic words and read them in bed the night before I left to fly back to England. They comforted me and confirmed my sense that what I was doing was not going off-piste or off my head. If anything my intention was to renew the pledges I had made to God by continuing to journey as I had initially promised when I first vowed poverty, chastity and obedience in the Divine service:

> *We slip our feet into the footprints of the Magi. We walk with them to the manger. We experience their shock and surprise as they find the epiphany that awaits them there. We offer our gifts with theirs.*
>
> *Then we do the bravest thing of all. We turn back with them. We set our faces to the new task, the new life that awaits us, a future that is quite unknown and quite precarious possibly. A future which is in God's gift, Amen.*

The process of leaving the IBVM was agonisingly simple. I saw the Provincial Superior; I saw her Council. When I think that it took me two-and-a-half years to join the community because our training as novices lasted that long, I was distressed that the dispensation from Rome came through in six weeks flat and landed on my doormat along with an advert for computer software and the gas bill. This is what it said:

> *The Congregation for Institutes of Consecrated Life and Societies of Apostolic Life, after careful consideration of the reasons submitted, grants the petition as requested.*

The petitioner is not to wear the religious habit any longer, and is separated from her institute.

The petitioner is to be aware that, according to canon 702, para 1, she cannot request anything from the institute for any work done in it. The institute, nevertheless, in accordance with canon 702, para 2, is to observe equity and evangelical charity towards her.

The rescript, unless it is rejected by the petitioner when it is communicated to her, brings with it a dispensation from vows and all obligations deriving from professio.

All things to the contrary notwithstanding.

Vatican, 21 January 2000

So that was that. When it wants to, Rome knows how to act promptly. The formula of the dispensation was simple. It defrocked me, dismantled any claims I might think I could make on the community for any emotional or financial recognition of thirty-six years of service and set me free. Only it was not as simple as that.

I had written a careful press statement on the day on which I said goodbye to the sisters. I had gone down to the Catholic Media Office near Westminster Cathedral to have it vetted by the staff there. After all I wanted to work with the system and not against it. Then I went back to Cambridge, to a word processor and a fax machine and issued four copies of the fax to the mainstream press. The next day all hell broke loose. I received over 160 telephone calls in eight hours flat. Every time I put down the telephone it would ring again and I would find that there were another eight or nine calls stacked up on call waiting, demanding to be answered. I was baffled. After all, I was not leaving the Catholic Church and had made that very clear. I was simply removing myself from my community so that I should no longer be a source of awkwardness to them in their dealings with the Vatican. I was making a bid for freedom in the sense that I was ensuring that if the Vatican did have anything to say to me, I should be in the direct line of fire. I should take the burden of their ire. I tried my best to answer the calls, to speak to the journalists and to offer interviews to the TV crews. At one moment there was an ITV crew in my upstairs study, setting up an interview for one telly news bulletins while another waited downstairs rigging up the sitting room for the nine o'clock news on BBC 1. This is sheer madness I thought, as I pulled the telephone connection out of the wall and smiled at the camera.

When the story broke in the newspapers, opinion among the punters was divided. There were those who sympathised with me. They wrote to me in great numbers. I received some 630 letters in the first month and tried to answer most of them. A friend came to help: a young woman who was expecting her first baby and who was skilled at slitting envelopes and ripping off the stamps. I composed a generalised answer and together we set about dealing with the mail. There were only three dissenting voices among my correspondents and I tried to answer them personally. The rest wrote letters which expressed personal distress at what had happened. Bishops and priests and seminary rectors wrote, as well as fellow religious and lay people. Some of the oldest and most unlikely sisters from my own community wrote immediately and comforted me greatly for what had happened. An elderly woman sent me four postage stamps. A couple sent me a ten-pound Boots token. Several people gave sums of money. I was bowled over by the weight of their sympathy. In fact I was overwhelmed by it.

So I changed my e-mail address immediately as I could not bear to turn on my computer and face fresh interest there. The new identity of a new e-mail address came as a fresh start. There is life after all of this, I decided. Only later did I bring myself to access the 268 e-mails which I received. Many of them were from IBVM sisters the world over expressing their contempt for Vatican strong-armed tactics. Many were from lay men and women who were baffled by the Vatican's apparent contempt for women, dressed up, as they saw it, in fancy language about their proper role and dignity. Many were from married people who were outraged that the contraception question was being kept alive in my case, whereas in their own it was a dead issue.

Among all these letters and e-mails there came one from a man I knew in the north of England, a former Anglican priest. He had been burrowing in a book while staying with a religious community. He copied his letter to the Catholic weekly, *The Tablet*, where it was duly published.

Sir, In the very same week that I read your report of Lavinia Byrne's resignation from the Institute of the

Blessed Virgin Mary, I was re-reading some notes I copied out a good while ago on the subject of the authority of an individual's conscience. I was surprised when my eyes fell on the following extract:

Over the pope as the expression of the binding claim of ecclesiastical authority, there still stands one's own conscience, which must be obeyed before all else, if necessary even against the requirement of ecclesiastical authority. This emphasis on the individual, whose conscience confronts him with a supreme and ultimate tribunal, and one which in the last resort is beyond the claim of external social groups, even of the official Church, also establishes a principle in opposition to increasing totalitarianism.

The truly astonishing thing is that these words, showing how the teaching of the Second Vatican Council on conscience was in the line of thought deriving from John Henry Newman, were written by none other than Joseph Ratzinger (in Herbert Vormgrimler, ed., Commentary on the Doctrine of Vatican II, *vol. v, p. 134) – now prefect of the Congregation for the Doctrine of the Faith, which Lavinia Byrne has experienced as 'pounding away' at her.*

Just how are these teachings and these actions compatible?

Dr Patrick Vaughan, Sheffield

At this time, *The Tablet* also published an article by Professor Nicholas Lash, the former Norris Hulse

Professor of Divinity in the University of Cambridge. It argued that we should consider the traditional doctrine of the 'reception' of official church teaching, namely the idea that Catholic teaching requires the 'echo' of assent from the faithful before it can claim to exist. 'Is not the whole Church indwelt by the Holy Spirit?' he asked. I found interventions like this incredibly consoling as they reminded me that there were other concerned people who were wrestling with the theological issues which I knew to be at stake.

Reactions in the secular press were totally predictable. The right-wing Catholic mafia came out in force and condemned me. I did not mind for myself, but I thought of the IBVM community and how much they would be suffering from the stupid posturing of these journalists. To comment on my appearance and to say that I took too much pride in my looks to wear a habit, for example, seemed to me contemptible. So much so that when I next went to see the man who cuts my hair at Reeds in Cambridge, it was I who had to end up comforting him on what he had read in an article by Paul Johnson's son in the *Daily Telegraph*. I found it baffling that my conscience should be dismantled in public by people who had not bothered to interview me and to hear my side of the story. To claim that I would expect to receive my pension and the royalties for my books from my former order when it is the state which pays our pensions and a publisher that handles my royalties was so much bunkum. Hitherto the community has received all the money I have earned since the age of seventeen; from now on, in the words of the dispensation from Rome, they are committed 'to observe equity and evangelical charity towards her' and I am confident that they will. Ditto the state; ditto the publishers.

With the journalists who did persevere with telephone calls and with whom I spoke personally, I had no problem. After all, they knew they were dealing with a real person as well as a news story. On a visit to Ireland where I had to give a paper at a conference a fortnight later, I spoke at length with Eileen Battersby from the *Irish Times* and admired her professionalism as she asked searching questions and made important connections. Gradually the dust settled.

Only, did it? What was going on? I have to say that I experienced a rush of energy and joy once I realised that the pressure to conform and to protect the reputation of other people was off me. Of course I miss the community. Of course I value the telephone calls and e-mails and the letters of those who are not intimidated and who keep up contact with me. I am not a pariah and do not intend to be one. I am sad and I am sorry, but I have no regrets.

There are practical results though. What happens to poverty, chastity and obedience when your reasons for keeping these commitments have changed and the context is no longer a community one? The vowed life remains important to me. The virtues you learn when you are accustomed to sharing what you have with other people do not go away. No day is complete if it does not begin with prayer, with the encounter with God which is the whole point of Christian discipleship, however it is configured.

Clearly there is gain and there is loss when you

leave a religious community for the reasons for which I had to leave mine. If, as I truly believe, the journey is my home, then I have to think about the next stage of the journey and about the next kind of home. I have been astonished by people's generosity in their interventions on my behalf. A friend had me to stay so that I could write part of this book. I had endless offers of hospitality and would have loved to take them all up had I not had work to do. I have taken time off, of course, and that has been used to go down to Somerset and to wander round looking for somewhere to live. My journey began there. If I were to choose to return there, it would not be in order to quit journeying but simply to have a better base to do it from.

I am beginning to identify things which I would like to do with the next stage of my life. One is to introduce a note of permanence and stability. I would love to garden, to put down roots and to get my hands dirty with something which feels healthy, namely with living soil, rather than with the detritus of a Vatican department which does not realise that its power to hurt and to harm reaches into people's very souls.

For of course I would like to see women ordained and of course I would like to see the Catholic Church rationalise its teachings on human sexuality in general and birth control in particular. I know that I am not alone in thinking these things and that, if they are God's will – as I believe they are – they will happen anyway.

I want to grow tomato plants and to watch the fruit ripening and reddening in the sun. I want to have a vine and a fig tree, to enjoy the fruitful harmony that the prophet Micah saw as the gift of God. I want to enjoy some serenity. These are very simple desires, but so too are the best things which we want from God and which God wants to give us. I would like to go on being able to say, 'I am and always have been a loyal daughter of holy mother Church' but, more importantly, it seems to me, and beyond any claims which the Church tries to make upon me, I am concerned to identify myself as a loyal daughter of God. Surely that is the greatest destiny of all. For if the journey is your home, your true homecoming can only be when your spirit finds its true rest in God.